ZILLAH'S GIFT

ZILLAH'S GIFT

LOIS WEST DUFFY

BEAVER'S POND
PRESS

ISBN 10: 1-59298-290-5
ISBN 13: 978-1-59298-290-5

Library of Congress Catalog Number: 2009930983
Printed in the United States of America
First Printing: 2009
13   12   11   10   09   5   4   3   2   1

Interior design by The Roberts Group
Cover design by Jay Monroe
Author photograph by Marilynn Johnson

BEAVER'S POND
PRESS

Beaver's Pond Press, Inc.
7104 Ohms Lane, Suite 101
Edina, MN 55439-2129
(952) 829-8818
www.BeaversPondPress.com

To order, visit www.BookHouseFulfillment.com or call 1-800-901-3480.
Reseller discounts available.

CONTENTS

CHAPTER 1

A MOTHER'S TOUCH

Uncle Mahli stomped across the compound of the caravanserai toward Zillah, sending little puffs of sand flying from under his sandals. His eyes were blazing, his face crimson with anger.

"I saw you scurrying to climb up there when you saw me coming, you lazy, good-for-nothing brat!" He shook his fist. "Why aren't those camels fed?"

Scrambling up the rocky path to where Zillah stood at her counting rock, he shouted, "You're slower and more worthless than your father was, that good-for-nothing brother I once had." He raised his fist in Zillah's face, but she stood firm and quiet, though his insults of her dead father cut like knives.

"Him with his dreaming and wandering off into the desert!" he raged. "If he'd stayed at his work instead of roaming around outside our walls, he'd be alive today. And I wouldn't be stuck with an ugly girl who is more trouble than she is worth."

Zillah was relieved when Uncle spat, cursed her, and turned to clamber back down the path and stalk away, anger radiating from his departing figure. Swallowing hard to get rid of the lump in her throat, she blinked to stop the hot tears from welling up in her eyes. She tried to remember things Father had said to make her laugh at Uncle's rages. But her memory of Father was already fading, though he had only died one year ago. She could no longer

1

remember exactly how his voice sounded, couldn't call up his silly laugh—Uncle used to say Father giggled like a girl. Zillah smiled at that thought. When Father laughed, it made everybody around him laugh, too, even those who didn't get the joke.

She hurried to arrange the small clay tablets before her on the flat black rock. These were more important than Uncle wanted to admit, for Zillah's tablets showed who came and went from the caravanserai compound, and how much they paid for sheltering there overnight. The surface of her black rock had been worn smooth by the hands of men like her father and grandfather who had kept the records before her.

A small girl with a tangled bush of black hair and deep brown eyes, Zillah was the first girl to work at the counting rock, and she was just tall enough to reach it. The sizzling desert heat was giving her a headache, and Zillah swiped her hand across her forehead. Pushing her hair back out of her eyes, she revealed a deep purple stain—a mark she'd had since birth—across her cheek.

Zillah looked up at the jagged mountains that framed the edges of her world, a walled compound in a valley of the Arabian Desert. Every caravan that crossed the desert followed the trail between these peaks. She shaded her eyes against the late-afternoon sun. A cloud of dust in the distance told her there would be a late arrival today.

She wondered what lay beyond what she could see. She could only guess from the goods that passed through the caravanserai: the precious stones, aromatic spices, and bright cloth the traders brought with them from the Orient, and the dried meat, fish, salt, gold, gems, and, sometimes, human slaves going East. Standing at her post, she could watch the travelers coming and going through both gates of the compound. But her big black rock was high enough to shield her from the stares of strangers. Her job was to keep track of every man and beast as well as everything they carried.

"Hey, Fishface!" came the jeering voice of young Kohath behind her. "What're you lookin' for, staring into those mountains?

Think someone's comin' to rescue you? Better get to work before your uncle grinds you up for camel fodder." He laughed at his own mean joke.

Kohath laughed again as Zillah instinctively raised her hand to cover the dark purple birthmark that flared across her left cheek and onto her neck. It was her first reaction when other children made fun of her, or when she met a stranger.

"Go away, Kohath!" Zillah cried. Remembering what her father had taught her, she added, "You're just mean and ignorant.

"When I was your age," she scolded, "I was already learning to count and read. You're big enough now to help feed the camels. If you can't even do that, then at least stay out of the way!"

Kohath only laughed again and sent a shower of stones her way, careful that they fell short. Even the son of the chief guard for the caravanserai wouldn't dare injure her, though his words were meant to wound. After all, her father had owned the caravanserai along with her Uncle Mahli. Though Uncle screamed at her and threatened her in front of everybody, they were all afraid of him.

Still, Kohath's words hurt more than stones. He was three years younger than her eleven years, but he echoed words he'd heard from bigger boys.

She remembered how the other children teased her about the strange dark mark on her face even when she was very small. They had invented the name Kohath used to taunt her: "Fishface." She had gone running to Father, who wiped away her tears and told her that not only her name, but also this special mark—her birthmark—had come from her mother.

"I gave you her name—Zillah—when she died," he said. "And she left this mark on your cheek when you were born, as a sign, so we would never forget her." Father sighed. "As though I ever could. When I look at you, I see the mark of her hand, a mark she left so you would know a mother's touch."

It was Father who taught her how to form the tablets from clay they dug from the riverbed then dried in the sun. Later, he taught her to count and showed her how to mark the numbers in the clay tablets with a camel-bone stylus that was as sharp as a knife. Uncle had complained that Father was wasting his time, teaching all this to a mere girl.

But with Father gone, how would Uncle's business survive if she hadn't learned to do this? No one else here knew how to read and write these numbers.

When she had finished this work, she jumped down and began the task of feeding the bawling camels. Kohath and the other boys were nowhere to be seen as she struggled to drag baskets of feed to where the camels groaned and pushed against each other and the sturdy wooden fence.

The biggest camel pushed its way up to the fence and snapped at her. Zillah jumped back in alarm as its big yellow teeth grazed her arm. She hurried to pour the green mulch of twigs and grass into the feeding trough, and then checked her arm. Good. No blood. The big animals were especially mean when they were hungry. Little rivers of sweat ran down Zillah's back, evaporating quickly in the dry desert heat. Dust was heavy in the air this afternoon, irritating Zillah's nose and making her eyes water. She sneezed, and the camel threw its head back and blared its ornery cry at her again, then turned, greedy, back to the fodder.

Guards armed with swords and heavy bows and arrows stood at various stations around the wall, keeping watch against anyone who might try to attack. Zillah glanced up at them, though they paid her no attention. As she watched, they raised the gates of the compound to admit a small, scraggly caravan of donkeys and their riders. They had not a camel among them, she noticed, wondering how they made it this far into the desert.

Late arrivals were the worst. The camels and donkeys were usually ill tempered from being driven hard to reach the compound before dark. But their owners paid handsomely for the protection the caravanserai offered, even more for water and food to carry them on their journey.

These new men and their animals ignored Uncle Mahli and

tried to rush past him to drink from the wells. They cursed at Uncle when he stood in their way. He shouted that they couldn't drink until they had been counted. Struggling to hold them back, he angrily shouted the numbers at Zillah. She kept her head down as she made her marks on the tablet so these troublesome new arrivals wouldn't see her face.

Although Kohath and the other boys were never around when there was work to do, they all showed up for loading and unloading cargo. They liked that job, watching for the chance to dip their thieving fingers into the packs. They stole small trinkets and food for themselves when they thought no one was watching. But Zillah's sharp eyes missed nothing, though she never dared to say anything.

Uncle Mahli was now strutting around to be sure everyone knew he was the head of the caravanserai. He held his head high, his filthy robes flapping around his ankles as he shouted more than he needed to at the guards, the workers helping to unload the animals' burdens, and Zillah. He was getting richer and richer from the steep tariffs he charged the traders for an overnight stay. Money was all that mattered to him.

Father had been so different from his stingy older brother. Everybody who came to the caravanserai liked him, with his pranks and stories. Camel drivers still asked about him.

Zillah worked hard each day, trying to fill her father's place in a way that would make him proud. She was careful to mark everything on the clay tablets because camel drivers didn't trust innkeepers and innkeepers didn't trust camel drivers, any more than they trusted the desert with its uncertain weather, bandits, and wild animals that could spring from nowhere. She was proud that Father had taught her to be honest as well as accurate in all that she did. The camel drivers were learning to trust her accounting.

Uncle Mahli often wanted her to add a few drachmas to the charge.

"It won't hurt. They won't miss it," he insisted. But he couldn't read what she marked down, so she did as she pleased.

CHAPTER 2

THE DESERT'S SECRET

Zillah loved the way her feet fit into the worn places in the rock where her father had stood, and his father before him. It made her feel closer to him and she liked that her growing feet were starting to fill the hollows where only men's feet had stood before.

Over the years, Zillah's family had expanded the walls, using camels to drag large rocks from the desert and stack them taller than the tallest man. Zillah's father showed her how much darker the original rocks were, so she could tell where the wall was new.

The main part of the settlement inside the walls was the long, low building made of brick and clay where travelers laid out their mats for sleeping. Travelers staying at the caravanserai ate their meals seated around the fire pit near its center. Their donkeys and camels were kept safe in a separate area, behind a fence made of small tree trunks fitted together so no animals could get in or out. The wells were the center of everything, the most important part of the entire compound and the most fiercely protected. The family's great-great-grandfathers had located these wells in the middle of the desert before memory, and the compound they built around them had supported the family for many generations.

Besides the rooms to lodge travelers, there was a cluster of small houses made of clay bricks. There, the guards and their families lived. Zillah and her father had lived with Uncle Mahli and Aunt Ahliah in a slightly bigger house, set apart from the others. Now Zillah had to stay there without the comfort of her father beside her.

Aunt Ahliah worked hard all day long, cooking for the travelers and directing the other women preparing food and tending the animals. Even Father had agreed that it was important for Zillah to learn this women's work. So she helped Aunt Ahliah as she cooked the meals, ground wheat for bread, and sewed garments from the cloth she bought from the traders.

As demanding as her work with the animals could be, Zillah preferred that to working within reach of Aunt's switch and her sharp tongue, especially now that she had no father to defend her.

Now Aunt called out to Zillah, interrupting her work at the black rock.

"Miserable girl, you will never be a proper wife if you don't learn your duties! There is work to be done here. You hide behind that rock, pretending to do the work of a scribe, while I need your help with the *real* work around here—the work that keeps a roof over your head and food in your belly."

Zillah sighed as she thought again that her aunt did not understand the "work of a scribe" as she called it. Where would she be without Zillah's numbers to ensure that people paid what they owed? But Aunt got even meaner when Zillah tried to finish up the count before answering.

"Now, Little Mouse, you think because your face is purple that you are royalty, when, in fact, that is a sign you are cursed to work even harder than others! Come and clean the pots before it's time to cook another meal!"

Zillah ignored the insult, but she rather liked the idea of her purple birthmark as a sign she was royalty. As she scrubbed the pots with sand before rinsing them in water, she daydreamed about her mother coming back as a queen, and Zillah herself as a princess whom Aunt Ahliah would have to obey.

Aunt Ahliah had given birth to two babies that Zillah could remember. But they both died before they learned to walk. Uncle Mahli blamed his wife because he had no sons to take on part of the work at the serai, and his wife was bitter that she had no daughters to share her burdens.

So it was Zillah she called, "Come, lazy girl, and get to work!"

"That's lazy *Zillah* to you, Aunt, or maybe Princess Zillah, if you please!" Zillah imagined herself answering, trying to make fun the way her father would, though Father said he felt sorry for Aunt Ahliah because her life was hard, too. He wanted a different life for Zillah.

Her dream was interrupted by a bellow from Uncle, "Where are you, stupid girl, when I need you at the gate?"

"If I'm so stupid, why is it I am the one who marks your records on the tablets?" she muttered, careful that he wouldn't hear. But she hurried to help him herd the animals into the holding pen.

"Tomorrow," she promised herself, "I'm going to take a walk in the desert, the way Father and I used to do after a really hard day." It was her favorite season, when the desert was in bloom. It was also the time to check on the most important secret of the desert that her father had taught her.

Father started taking Zillah along on his short trips into the desert as soon as she could walk. He showed her how to mark her way, paying attention to specially shaped rocks, like the one he called "the camel's nose," that could guide her back to the caravanserai. As they walked along, he pointed out the signs of little desert animals like the peccaries that ran in herds. He said that they could be as mean as camels, but quicker. He taught her to watch for scorpions, spotting their subtle tracks in the sand. He helped her find hidden water in the early morning before it evaporated, water she could drink from little hollows in the rocks.

It was on these explorations that he showed her how to dig down to the wet clay beside the desert stream to make the counting tablets and to form little clay jugs with plugs. The jugs were part of their great secret—the secret that would some day buy their freedom from Uncle Mahli's harsh control.

To protect her and the secret, her father had shown her a roundabout way to their destination. "I'm going to show you a rare and special tree, and I don't want anyone following us to see where we are headed," he'd said.

Her father guided her around a large outcropping of rock, and she realized she could no longer see their compound. As they climbed higher, she caught sight of home again, but then it disappeared at the next turn.

Father told her to walk slowly and carefully, watching so she would miss nothing. Zillah was thrilled to see the delicate beauty of small yellow flowers she might have overlooked, and rocks so small and milky white she wanted to put them in her pockets to take them home. Father told her, "No, the rocks belong to the desert." But he smiled and added, "If you learn to know the desert as I show you, it can become your home as well as the caravanserai, and all the rocks will belong to you. And you can be almost as safe."

At last they made their way over a great black mound. Below them was a wide, curved wadi, a gully with a very small stream running through it. The stream ran only during the rainy season, her father said, pouring through the rocks and down into the gravelly wadi. Below the stream Zillah saw a patch of green surrounding several rough-barked trees with rugged, gnarly branches and yellow-green leaves. Where she and her father stood, both they and the trees were in a rocky hollow quite hidden from the traders' road. Father sighed with pleasure.

As they walked toward the trees, the air was filled with a sharp sweetness, like the fruits and flowers of springtime all collected in one place. There was the tang of the lemons some of the traders from the East brought through the caravanserai from time to time. Zillah had never tasted one, but the bright yellow color and the keen fragrance always attracted her.

When they reached the trees, Father showed her how to make

cuts in the bark of the trees so that they oozed drops of a fragrant oil that he said would only come at this time of year. He collected the oil in one of the small jugs they had made.

"Traders will pay dearly for this oil," he explained. "Some will stop at nothing to find out where we get it. So we must be very careful about offering it to a trader. It will have to be someone we know well. And you must never, ever show anyone where to find these trees."

After collecting all the oil they could get from the trees in the new jug, they would hurry back to the caravanserai. Once there, they added the jug to the small collection of clay jugs, which they had hidden among towering rocks just inside the south gate to the caravanserai. It was a good hiding place, easy for them to watch over and not likely for others to search.

After Father died, no one but Zillah knew this secret.

CHAPTER 3

DANGER
IN THE DESERT

Zillah was up at first light to creep out the door and into the chilly desert morning before anyone else was awake. Once the bustle of preparing food for the travelers was under way, no one would miss her. Aunt would be angry, but would think Zillah was working with the animals. Uncle would think she was helping Aunt.

When she was sure no one was watching, she made her way to the south gate. There, she carefully checked the small oil jugs huddled in their hiding place, making sure they were still safe. Then she slipped out the gate.

Following the markings of the desert she knew so well, she moved quickly off the traders' trail and over the rocky hill toward the treasured trees. She watched for any sign of life—a desert creature or a traveler about at this early hour. She heard sounds of life all around her, but when she was quiet, they all became quiet, too.

"That's how I must be," Zillah thought, "giving away nothing of my presence."

She was careful to leave no sign of her passing, not even a footprint, stepping only on rocks or where tough desert grass grew, springing back after she passed.

13

This was her first trip to the secret trees since her father's death—her first without him. As she walked the trail, she would pass the caves where the bodies of the dead were buried, she stopped to pick some desert flowers and laid them at the mouth of the caves.

"Spirit of my father," she prayed as she went on her way, "watch over me today as I go in search of our oil trees. I promise to be careful and to keep them a secret. But you have to protect me."

When she got to the bluff above the perfumed oil trees, she sat down and looked around her, pretending she had nothing on her mind but play, just in case someone was watching her. Seeing and hearing nothing, she made her way to the first tree. She was happy to find the spot, just as she remembered it.

Following Father's instructions, she carefully cut a hole through the tree's bark and teased the small drops of oil into her clay jar. Pleased with herself, she did the same thing at each tree until her little jar was nearly full. It was a good year for oil!

She was careful as she plugged the jar and placed it in the leather pouch hanging from her waist. She didn't spill a single drop. Then she turned to go back to the caravanserai. Her father would have been proud, she thought.

As she turned toward home, she thought back to the day, much like today, when her father had stolen out into the desert before dawn, while Zillah and Aunt and Uncle were still sleeping. The day he didn't come back.

He often went out, telling Uncle Mahli he was watching for signs of trouble. Once she was old enough to make the early-morning journeys, he usually took her with him. At least, he would wake her and tell her where he was going. But on this day, she was startled to awaken and find her father was gone. She searched outside, where other men from the caravanserai gathered in the shade of a tree, preparing to drink their strong, sweet morning tea. But he wasn't there.

"Have you seen my father?" she asked. "Do you know where he went?"

One of the younger men mocked her, imitating in a singsong voice, "Have we seen your father? Do we know where he went?" He dipped his finger in his tea to draw an outline like her birthmark on his own cheek and made a sour face.

"Of course, we haven't seen your father," he said. "He goes where he pleases."

Zillah looked all around the caravanserai, at last walking along every wall, peering out the gates. She worked her way to the south gate where she checked their stash of oil jars. She was a little afraid her father might have gone away without her, perhaps to sell the oil to buy a better life. She was relieved to see them still safe in their hiding place.

But as the morning passed, she grew more and more uneasy. She was afraid to go out into the desert by herself to search for him. There were so many places he could have gone—and she wasn't sure she could find her way back without him. At one turn, she felt hopeful, thinking, "I know he's found the sweet-sap tree, and he would want me to bring some of the clay jars we made to gather the oil." Then she felt despair: "Maybe someone has carried him away, and he needs me to rescue him. But I'll need help!"

When she couldn't stand it any longer, she tried to steal unseen out the gate of the serai in search of him. She wanted to believe she would find him at the secret tree, gathering new stores of the precious oil.

But Aunt Ahliah caught sight of her and shouted, "You sneak! Where do you think you're going? Come back and get to work!"

Almost relieved to have her decision made, Zillah turned back to the familiar morning chores.

The men ate their morning meal and still her father had not appeared. Uncle Mahli grumbled about it, "He has no regard for me and the heavy burden I carry! Our father trusted this oasis to the two of us, but my brother would rather wander in the desert than tend to business."

As the morning wore on, everyone began to worry about Zillah's missing father. But no one more than Zillah.

In the late afternoon, some travelers leading a donkey approached the caravanserai from the west. They looked serious and sad. One of their donkeys carried a large bundle wrapped in a cloth stained the unmistakable red of blood. Uncle Mahli shoved Zillah aside as he rushed to meet the travelers. Everyone from the serai gathered in silence, almost as if they knew what the travelers would say.

"We found this man's body, lying on a pile of rocks not far from here," one of the men explained. "No one was around, so we wrapped him in this cloth and brought him here."

"We felt the danger!" another man blurted. "It must have been bandits, and they might have been waiting for us or for another caravan!"

A third man, a big ugly man in a red turban who didn't seem to be part of the group, spoke up, flashing his saber, "They wouldn't dare argue with my knife! I'd soak the desert sand with their blood!"

Uncle Mahli rushed to the body and pulled the cloth from around the head. Then he began to wail and pound his chest. "By the gods!" he raged. "Why, why did you go into the desert alone? How many times did I tell you, 'Stay where you are safe, with your family around you!' But no! You had to go into the desert today, when there are thieving, murderous bandits about!" He put his head in his hands.

Uncle's outburst shocked Zillah. She could hardly take it all in. It had to be a mistake. Why did Uncle think the body was that of his brother, her father? It couldn't be!

Zillah made her way to the body now lying on the ground. One glimpse and she knew her uncle told the truth. It was, indeed, her father's face, still and pale except for the blood caked across his face and in his hair. She threw herself upon him, weeping and calling out, "Father! Father! You have to be alive! Talk to me, Father! Tell me you won't leave me!" But his pale lips were still and covered with sand.

One of the travelers pulled at Zillah's shoulder and tried to lift her away from her father's side. But Zillah refused to be moved, her tears falling on Father's face and in his hair. She sat beside him, holding his head in her lap as the sun rose higher in the sky. Others in the serai stood back.

In the buildings behind her, Zillah heard the women's voices raised in the death wail. At last Aunt Ahliah came to her and scolded, "Zillah, you can't change life or death by your stubborn ways. Your father's body is all that is left of him. You cannot keep it here in the middle of the serai. We must prepare it for burial. Now move, so we can get on with what must be done."

Zillah stood, feeling empty and alone, her tears now dry. What would become of her? Where would she go? How would she live? How could she stay with Uncle and Aunt without Father and his jokes? Who would look out for her?

But there was little time for grieving. Uncle Mahli jerked Zillah's arm and pointed her in the direction of the black rock where her father always worked. "Go! Take your father's place. There is too much for one man to do, even one as strong and clever as I."

When she didn't move, he pushed her toward the rock that had been her father's station. It was hers now.

As she walked away from the burial cave, tears blurred her vision, but she didn't care. The aching memory of her father helped fill the emptiness. Suddenly, she felt a different kind of movement around her. She automatically crouched where she was, making herself small behind a flowering cactus plant, every sense alert.

CHAPTER 4

A CLOSE CALL

She smelled him first. A man who didn't fit in the desert. Just over the next ridge. He carried a walking stick, and a heavy coating of dust clung to his fine clothes. He looked too rich to be traveling alone—a sure target for bandits. He was big and round, and as he drew closer, she saw his wide red nose and squinty eyes that looked as though they could hardly see around the big nose. He wore a strange red turban and layers and layers of fine fabric to protect him from the desert heat. He seemed to be looking for something. Zillah hardly dared to breathe as he walked out of sight and over a nearby hillock.

It wasn't smart to call attention to himself. He was either new to the desert or he didn't worry about attackers. Then she saw that he wore an impressive saber tied around his waist. Nearby, on top of a stand of rocks, were several rough-looking men who wore dark turbans like the other man's red one. Zillah's skin prickled and every muscle in her body tensed.

Was he the red-turbaned man who showed up at the serai when her father was killed? What was he doing here?

She ducked behind a shield of bushes, unsure which way to turn. She hoped she knew more about the desert than these men, and that she could outsmart them. She crouched low and, watching them all the while, circled around to get behind them.

Suddenly, one of the men turned, spotted her, and shouted out to the others. Zillah froze, terrified as they came rushing after her. But once she started moving, her feet were sure while the men clearly hadn't learned to run in the desert. She zigzagged this way and that, trying to duck out of sight wherever possible. But their shouts told her they weren't far behind.

She was horrified to realize that she was running toward the secret trees and turned aside. Then she realized that the treasured oil might be what they were looking for.

The men were gaining on her, and Zillah turned past a huge rock and ducked over the next ridge. There was the ancient wildcat trap! Her father had told her of this place where her ancestors had set traps to capture the wild desert cats, which they then killed and ate for food. It appeared to be a pile of rocks. But Zillah knew that hidden in the pile was a long and dark passage, the place where the wildcat would be trapped once it took the bait and a rock slammed down across the entrance of the opening. She hesitated—she couldn't see the end of the passage—then made a desperate dive for the hollow space. It was a risk, but the men who chased her weren't desert-wise, so they might not see it. Besides, they were too big to crawl in after her, though they might block the entrance if they saw her go inside.

Her heart was pounding so that she was afraid the men might hear it. She tried to silence her breathing as she heard them run past. They cursed loudly as they ran so she was able to hear them leaving, heading away from her hiding place and searching where they would not find her or the oil trees. She huddled there for a long time, waiting until she could no longer hear the men's voices or their scuffling feet. Still, she worried that they might be lurking nearby.

When at last Zillah made her way back to the caravanserai, she knew Uncle would be furious with her—and Aunt, too. She had missed the morning meal and her stomach hurt, whether from hunger or fear, she didn't know.

As she expected, Kohath greeted her, a smirk on his face. "You're gonna get it this time. Your uncle is looking for you, and he's not happy!"

When she turned the corner to find Uncle Mahli, she saw that he was talking to the ugly stranger in the red turban. Both men saw her at the same time. The stranger looked at her and rubbed his hands together, his dark eyes darting around the compound. As she got closer, she could see he was even greasier and dirtier than she thought. She saw him offer a scrawny goat to Uncle, who called to Zillah in a sweet, wheedling voice she knew not to trust.

"My dear child . . ." he said, as she walked toward him. She was cautious, her step too slow for him, and his voice turned hard as he called out to her again. "Step it up, girl. You are especially slow today." Then he turned back to the ugly stranger, speaking again in that wheedling tone.

"No, no," she heard him say. "She is the only child of my dear dead brother, and I could never sell her so cheaply." He placed his heavy hand on Zillah's head, pulling her hair to make her turn around. She pulled back in disgust as he traced her birthmark with his dirty thumb.

"And you see, she carries an unusual curse. To have that curse under your power, you would need to pay many goats. More than you have."

Zillah knew that some people who came through the caravanserai saw her birthmark as an evil sign from the gods. Those superstitious people wouldn't let their children or animals near her. Uncle often used that false notion when it suited his purposes, but it filled her with rage. She looked at the greasy trader and wrinkled her nose in disgust. Then she spat at his feet, careful not to actually hit him, and walked away.

Uncle Mahli grabbed her shoulder and jerked her around, then slapped her face. "You will not be disrespectful! Now go back and draw water for those camels!" He gave her a rough shove and told the red-turbaned stranger, "Ask me another day, and I might

21

sell her cheaply. I might even pay you to take her." He gave a short, harsh snort and stomped across the dusty ground.

The stranger smiled at her. It wasn't a real smile. It meant nothing good. He rubbed his hands together again and stared as she walked away. She walked as fast as she could but would not run. She felt sure he was thinking of the oil trees. She wanted to appear strong and unafraid.

Zillah turned to her work, wiping angry tears from her cheeks so the men wouldn't see them. She would never let Uncle know how much he hurt her. Never! As for trying to fetch a pretty price by selling her to that greasy trader—Zillah shivered in disgust. She would run away first, take her chances in the desert. Rats in the desert must have a better life than hers.

CHAPTER 5

A WONDROUS STAR

The caravanserai had never been busier. Zillah barely had time to finish registering one caravan before another appeared at the gate. Large and small, the caravans came, many of them travelers that Zillah had never seen.

She watched for the greasy trader and his men for awhile, then all but forgot about them in the rush. Once in a while she glanced toward the south gate where her small treasure of precious oil was hidden, but she hardly even had time for that.

Many travelers talked of the Roman ruler, Caesar Augustus. He had given an order for all his subjects in the vast Roman Empire to be counted and to pay a tax. Even though there were many differences in the languages spoken by the travelers, Zillah heard grumbling in all of their voices. She understood enough of their words to know that the people felt oppressed, burdened.

But the travelers had to be careful because the Romans had ears everywhere. If people complained too much, or too loudly, the Roman king would take their property, or maybe even kill them. Some of the travelers were Jews, and she heard that they were constantly afraid for their lives. As she listened to their stories, she was glad that she and her family were Elamite and that the Roman king wasn't after them.

But more than the movement of people, a new and more un-usual sign appeared that both awed and puzzled Zillah.

Father taught her to watch everything around her, even the sky for signs of changing weather or seasons. Most of the people at the caravanserai never bothered to lift their eyes from the ground, so no one else was watching the changes in the night sky. She had no one to talk to about the marvel that now appeared each evening: a new star, growing brighter each night, until it was the most bril-liant star in the clear night sky. The light from the star seemed to reach down to touch the very tops of the nearby mountains. Sometimes Zillah felt as though she could reach out and feel the soothing warmth of its glow on her skin.

Before long, she found herself waiting for the sun to go down every day so she could see this wondrous star. Yet, she wondered why neither travelers nor people living in the caravanserai talked about it. Did no one else see it? And why was it now in their sky? She wished Father were here to explain it to her.

By nightfall, most everyone else in the compound tumbled quickly onto their sleeping mats, many of the men drunk from wine. The women's quarreling voices gradually gave way to silence.

Zillah was startled out of her thoughts one evening by the shrill voice of Aunt Ahliah calling for her to come and help draw water for a late caravan. She had been so busy gazing at the sky that her attention had wandered and she missed this new group's arrival. It was unusual for caravans to arrive after dark.

"Yes, Aunt, I hear you," she sighed.

Above the animal calls and the shouts of their drivers, Zillah heard Uncle shouting furiously, "Girl! Girl! Where are you?" Zillah shrugged in frustration—it was impossible to satisfy both her aunt and her uncle. Her aunt might beat her when she didn't answer her call, but Aunt's beatings were not as hard as Uncle Mahli's, and never lasted so long. Finally, she ran toward the new caravan com-ing through the gates.

Zillah was amazed at the splendor of this new caravan. She had never seen anything quite like it. The camels were bigger than most, beautiful and well cared for. Their coats were brushed and shiny, not like the filthy beasts of burden that normally came through the gates. Yet, it was evident that this caravan came from far away because of the heavy coating of dust on the outer clothing of the camel drivers whose cloaks were more colorful than any that had ever come to the caravanserai.

Zillah counted forty-nine camels as the caravan and its passengers, guards, and drivers crowded into the serai. Three of the camels carried large covered platforms she had learned were called howdahs. When the camel drivers commanded the camels to kneel, three exotic-looking princes stepped out of the howdahs, dressed in clothing of such magnificence it made her blink.

Golden chains and unusual jeweled charms encircled the neck of each animal. And each richly robed prince was accompanied by beautiful women, also dressed in fine clothing embroidered in rich colors that shone like a desert sunrise. Their jewels sparkled in the starlight, and there was a fragrance about them that even the nasty smell of the camels couldn't hide.

As Zillah drew closer, she saw that each prince wore a unique gold ring. And each wore a garment of silk and linen in a different color from the others—one in a red so deep it was almost purple, one in an astonishing shade of yellow ochre, and one in a brilliant green with rich gold embroidery. All about them were armed guards, wearing swords and knives, their eyes moving all the time, taking in everything and everyone in the serai.

Even their servants wore clothing woven of one cloth with no tears or patches. Almost everyone in the desert wore patched clothing, since the sand quickly wore down even the strongest cloth.

Over the years, Zillah had listened and learned to understand words of many different languages spoken by the travelers, though she knew not to share this knowledge with Uncle. But these strangers spoke in tongues she had never heard. She strained to understand, trying to learn something about them as she approached the caravan.

As always, she kept her head down and turned slightly away, ashamed of the purple mark on her face. She held out her clay tablet to show that she was ready to register the newcomers.

Uncle was already urging her to hurry. "Where have you been, Baggage? You're never where I need you." His face was the red it usually was when he was angry.

These strangers looked from one to another, puzzled at what they saw—the angry man and the browbeaten girl assigned to record their arrival. They clearly didn't expect to do business with a young girl.

The handsome camels carried bulging leather bags, and Zillah wondered what such bags might contain. She saw Uncle eyeing them greedily, but it was her job to register them. "He'll sneak around to look for himself," she thought, and vowed to keep an eye on him.

"Welcome, travelers, to our caravanserai," Uncle said in that syrupy voice he used with strangers—especially wealthy ones such as these. Already Zillah knew that he would press his stubby fingers on the back of her neck, a sign that he wanted her to add an extra charge on the tariff these visitors would pay.

Because she could see that these strangers had come from far away, Zillah was surprised when the tallest, the man in red, began to speak in the familiar tongue of the serai.

"Would you please show us where we could all find water? We have traveled a great distance, and we are very thirsty. Our animals, too, need water. After that, you may begin to mark down our camels and our cargo, for we are many and we still have far to go."

With a stern look at Uncle Mahli, he added, "We will pay you what the stay is worth, but no more."

Before Uncle could object, Zillah led them to the well, where wooden buckets waited to be lowered into the water. The tall prince turned to several boys and directed them to help her with the buckets. Kohath, as usual, was nowhere to be seen when there was work to do.

"Surely, you are not expected to lift this water for the animals all by yourself!" the prince exclaimed. "Where are the grown women or the young men who do this chore?"

"I may look small to you, but I am very strong," Zillah boasted. But the kindness in his voice was almost too much for her—harder to bear than Uncle's harsh voice and cutting words. She felt the tears rise in her eyes, ready to brim over, and she lowered her head to hide them. The prince seemed not to notice the purple mark on her face.

"Please, would you tell me your name?" the stranger asked. Zillah had never been treated with such courtesy. And no one had ever asked her name. In fact, no one ever *asked* her for anything. They demanded her services, the water she poured and the errands on which she was sent.

"My name is Zillah," she answered, "daughter of Malek, late of this desert caravanserai." She liked saying her name aloud, and her father's. Uncle Mahli always called her "girl" or something worse like "baggage." He never, ever, used her name, and neither did Aunt Ahliah.

"Zillah," said the stranger smiling. "A good, strong name for a strong, smart girl."

A rough hand on Zillah's shoulder pulled her away from the stranger. Uncle hissed in her ear, "No time for your chattering. See those camels and goats to feed? And you need to bring wood for the fire. Are you forgetting your duties? You think that because you can read and write you are better than the rest?"

Turning to the stranger, he simpered, "We are here to serve you."

"Never mind," said the stranger. "We have cooks who will prepare the food to which we are accustomed for our evening meal. But we will gladly use the fire pit over there." He called out, in his own language, to his servants.

The other two princes joined him. The one dressed in ochre was the shortest, his strong, dark, bare arms circled with thick bracelets of gold. The other prince had fine features and wisps of golden hair, which rested on the green cloak that covered him from head to toe.

"We will stay until tomorrow afternoon, and will travel by night after a rest," the tallest prince said. The other two nodded in agreement.

"At night! But you can't! There are bandits. You—your—sirs, if I may say so, you appear even to the eyes of a simple man like myself to possess riches that will be an invitation to desert thieves. Such a call they hear a thousand oases away!" Uncle Mahli was so excited he was almost choking on his words, and his hands and arms jerked nervously.

The three princes smiled at one another and then at Uncle Mahli. The one in green spoke for the first time. "Thank you, sir, for your concern. But we are well guarded. We are traveling by the light of a special star—you may have seen it in the evening sky— and bandits want no part of us because of it."

He turned his face toward the sky. "Look!" he commanded.

He was pointing to the brilliant star Zillah had seen. It was now so bright that she had to shield her eyes. Even Uncle gasped when he saw it. The gathering evening seemed to fall away, and it was like daylight again. Zillah turned to her tasks, helped by the light of the star. She hurried through her work, hoping for a chance to ask the visitors why they followed the star.

CHAPTER 6

THE THREE MAGI

The caravan seemed to fill the entire compound. The other travelers moved to the outer edges, in awe of these exotic people and their ways. Even with so many people crowded into the serai, there was a peace such as Zillah had never experienced. No one quarreled, and the workers didn't even raise their voices at one another. She herself found that she didn't notice how tired she was nor did she mind the extra work. Only Aunt Ahliah seemed unaware of the peace and continued calling irritably for Zillah.

Meanwhile, the servants from the exotic caravan built their fire in the center of the compound and hurried about, preparing food and caring for the animals. The fragrance of the spices in the food cooking over the fire made Zillah's mouth water. But there was no time to check to see what the food looked like or to enjoy the smells because Aunt Ahliah was so demanding.

Zillah finished the registrations, then directed the servants to the holding pens for their animals. They traveled prepared for everything, Zillah thought, as she watched how carefully they handled the animals. In fact, even as travelers, their lives and those of the animals were better than that of the innkeeper and his family.

She wondered if the people in this strange caravan were always as kind as they seemed, as she hurried to set out the bread and dried goat meat that would be the evening meal for Aunt and

Uncle. They were all too tired to cook over a fire when night came. Zillah was allowed to eat what was left.

Although she was very sleepy, Zillah's curiosity drew her to the edge of the unusual royal caravan after Uncle and Aunt had fallen asleep on their mats. The amazing star was still overhead, so she could see everything as though it were daylight. She hung back in the shadows so they wouldn't see her.

The three leaders of the group gathered on a little hill, a group of their menservants around them. They set up big, complicated instruments such as Zillah had never seen. Some of the men set tall sticks in the ground, then measured the shadows by stepping them off. They made notations on pieces of tanned calfskin rather than clay tablets as Zillah always used. They used burnt sticks to make their marks.

When they pointed their instruments to the sky, Zillah thought it might be some kind of magic. Were they trying to call the wondrous star down from the sky or learn what message it might be sending earthward? She was startled when one of the women noticed her and beckoned her to sit on a soft, colorful wool shawl she spread on the ground. Although she was still a little afraid, Zillah joined the other women to watch as the princes went about their work.

Zillah studied the women around her, to see how she should behave. She didn't feel as though she fit in at all. Because she was afraid they would notice the birthmark, she lifted her scarf over her face. If she got too close, the women might cry out and send her away as superstitious travelers had done before. She moved forward to join them, but she was ready to jump and run at any minute.

To her surprise, one of the older women spoke to her, not in their strange tongue but in Zillah's own. Zillah had never known another woman to speak in more than one tongue.

"Young Zillah, please come and join us, and we will tell you the story of the star we follow," the woman said. "It is a very special one."

The woman began to talk as the others gathered around.

"Long ago, in a distant hill country," the woman began, "long before you were born, Zillah—even before I was born—our fathers began to read signs in the stars. Those signs and ancient stories, which were passed down through the ages, predicted the birth of a new king. A star would lead the way to this new king, and he would be king of the Jews." Zillah paid close attention, and as she listened, the walls of the serai seemed to fall away. She imagined herself in that far distant time.

"This was not happy news for our people," the woman went on. "The Jews were a mighty people known as the Nation of Israel. They were wandering tribes who moved into new lands at the direction of a mighty god who, they said, gave them power over these lands. And they were so successful that our fathers were afraid of them.

"So they spied on these Israelites to see how they could win battles even when they were overpowered and outnumbered. They saw that the Israelites worshipped one god, and one only, and they claimed that their power came from that god. That's why the Romans watch them carefully, even now."

The woman stopped and looked at Zillah, who shivered a little as she stared back. She had never heard of these long-ago battles, and she knew nothing of the god of the Jews. Traders coming through the serai from all directions talked of this god or that, and Zillah took it all in. She would sometimes pray to one of the gods she heard mentioned, but it never seemed to make a difference. After her father was killed, she prayed to his spirit, and sometimes to the rocks or trees where they had walked together. That sometimes helped her feel safer, but she wasn't sure she should trust that feeling.

She had seen men who were called Romans and listened to their talk at the caravanserai. Their soldiers were proud and arrogant, and people stayed out of their way. But she was more afraid of the desert bandits, who were more real to her than any god, for they had taken Father from her.

Thinking of her father made her feel sad, and she pulled up her knees to rest her cheek on them. The woman sitting beside her wrapped a shawl around her, one that smelled of desert flowers and felt soft and smooth next to Zillah's skin. Zillah rubbed her hand over it to feel the softness.

A young girl put in her hand a small clay jar filled with a hot liquid that smelled of sweet spices. Zillah held it gratefully between her shaking hands, enjoying both the scent and the warmth, but she was afraid to open her mouth to drink it. When she finally took a small taste, it was strong and spicy and tasted very good.

"Here is my daughter, Siri, bringing you bread," the storyteller said. "Here. Eat." Siri placed a warm crust of bread in Zillah's hand.

Zillah took another small taste of the drink in her hand, then gulped it down, even though she still didn't know what it was. It seemed to her that the bread and the warm drink were more delicious than anything she had ever tasted. Now her belly was filled with warmth, and she was grateful. She had been hungrier than she had realized with all the excitement.

"Our leaders, the three Magi, are royal astrologers," the woman explained. "They always study the heavens for new signs as the seasons change. The stars that guide our lives are full of mysteries the Magi seek to unravel. This strange new star that moves ahead of us is the key to the biggest mystery.

"It appears that a new king is to be born under the rule of the Romans, but he is to be born among the Jews," she went on.

"Are your people still afraid?" Zillah asked.

"No," the woman answered. "As they studied the signs in the heavens, our leaders came to understand that they had nothing to fear from this new king. And because his birth is important enough to be announced in this way, they decided to find him and pay their respects. They believe that many will seek him for his peace and wisdom."

"But why was that star revealed first to your people? Who are you, and who are your people? And why are your leaders called Magi?" Zillah asked.

The woman smiled. "My name is Jorai. We are Assyrian. We come from three small kingdoms, each headed by these three Magi named Balthazar, Kaspar, and Melchoir. Each was assigned a kingdom to lead because of his powers of discernment and wisdom," Jorai said. "You may have noticed that each wears the color of his kingdom.

"My family and I belong to the kingdom of Balthazar—the tall one in red. The one in ochre is Kaspar. That shade of yellow ochre is the royal color of his kingdom, which is just over the mountain from ours. He is a man of great strength. It would take a brave man, indeed, to cross him. But he hides that under laughter and the stories he tells, so everyone is drawn to him. Melchoir, in the green and gold, is from the kingdom just next to ours. He speaks little, but he is also very wise. He understands the messages of the stars better than anyone.

"These kingdoms are small but secure, for the Magi rule well, with guidance from the stars and from wisdom passed down from their mothers and fathers before them. Still, everyone is curious about this new king. He is called the Prince of Peace, and the stories of the seers are that he will set his people free."

"Is that what the great star is telling you? That the Jews will finally be free of the Romans? That we will all be free? Even the slaves?" Zillah asked.

It was so confusing. Jorai's story seemed little more than a jumble of words in her ears, though it was in her own tongue. She wondered if that could possibly mean that she could be set free from Uncle and Aunt, even though she was neither Jew nor Assyrian.

"All we know is that the Magi say that the bright star will show us where to find this new king," Siri said. "They make new charts each evening when the star is brightest. That's what they are doing now."

CHAPTER 7

ZILLAH'S SIGN

Zillah and Siri crept closer to where Balthazar, Kaspar, and Melchoir gazed into the instruments pointed at the sky. Their charts and maps were spread on the ground. Kaspar and Melchoir made lines and circles in the sand that they measured with more strange instruments.

Zillah was startled by a voice just behind them, hissing, "What do you think you're doing? Girls have no business here!"

But Siri didn't act surprised or afraid. "Be quiet, Zothar!" she whispered. "We have as much right to be here as you do!"

"Everyone knows girls are unclean if they haven't been purified," he said with a sneer. "What do we know of this strange girl beside you? She is foreign to our ways."

Zillah kept her head down and turned aside so the owner of the voice—this Zothar—would not see her face and cause more trouble. It was one thing to be sent away because they were girls—they could always sneak back. But the moment someone decided Zillah and her purple mark were a curse, she wouldn't be allowed anywhere near the others.

Out of the corner of her eye, she watched the boy who spoke. He was older than she—probably about the age of Siri, who seemed several years older than Zillah. They hadn't noticed him as they crept nearer to the Magi. Zothar, too, was skulking around the edges of the Magi's work, trying to watch. Siri turned her back, ignoring him, so Zillah did the same, even though it made her uneasy not to keep an eye on him.

As the Magi concentrated even more intensely on the heavens, Zillah crept closer, forgetting both Zothar and Siri. She wanted desperately to see what they saw, to know what they knew. She was looking so hard that she didn't see Melchoir, step back. He tripped over her small form and almost fell.

"By the gods!" he swore softly. Zillah cringed and scrambled backward, but Melchoir looked at her more closely and his face softened.

"So you are curious, young Zillah." He beckoned. "Come, I'll show you." Too late, Zillah noticed that both Zothar and Siri had kept a respectful distance, as had the other women and most of the men as well.

Her fears that Melchoir would see her birthmark as a curse melted as he showed no sign that he noticed. He guided her to the instrument and showed her how to move her head until her eye could see what he had seen.

At first, she saw nothing; then she gasped as the sky came into focus. She saw stars so close she thought she could reach out and touch them.

"This is magic!" she said. "You bring the stars down to earth!"

Melchoir laughed kindly. "No, it only looks that way," he said. "It took me long years to develop this instrument to help us see the heavens. That's how we located the great star before anyone else." He seemed proud and eager to explain his invention, even to a young girl.

"If you could look at our ancient charts, you would see that no such star graced the heavens before now," he explained. "Many moons past, we began to see a strange new light and identified it as this star. We kept the news to ourselves, for we did not know what meaning such a star could have. It could have meant good for our kingdoms, or it could have meant disaster.

"As the moons came and went, the star seemed to come closer

to the earth. We thought everyone could see it. But no other seers came forth," he explained. "Then, just when we feared it was coming to destroy the earth, it stopped moving closer. But it kept growing brighter.

"Then two of the brightest stars seemed to meet with this new star in the constellation Pisces, The Fish, to form a single brilliant star. And so, as it began to move through the sky, we believed we should follow.

"We quickly gathered our camels, the servants, and supplies to last many moons. As we follow, the star has been moving quickly, leading us over mountains and plains, past seas and rivers, but never so fast that our camels and donkeys cannot follow."

"But I never saw this star until just before you came to the caravanserai!" Zillah exclaimed.

"This star is not visible to everyone when it is visible to us," answered Balthazar, who had walked over to join them. "And we are not sure why."

The wise men showed her how they plotted their course, following wherever the star led. Zillah was excited to see how they traveled across the high mountains and the mysterious desert without seeking the paths beaten by other feet for centuries.

"You will be a wise woman one day," Balthazar told her, as he watched her study the charts.

"You have already learned more than most, in knowing how to mark down the cargoes that come through the gates of this caravanserai. We have traveled far, and we have not seen a young girl who is as eager to learn as you are."

"Besides," Balthazar added, "you had already seen the star before we arrived. Your eyes had already been opened."

Instinctively, Zillah put her hand to her face, fearing they might see her mark in the bright light of the star and send her away.

But Balthazar touched her cheek lightly and traced the outline of the birthmark. His touch was gentle, like that of her father. No one else had ever dared to touch her mark.

"Do not fear, Zillah, for the mark sets you apart," he said.

"Come and look through the lens once more. I'll show you why this mark is not a thing to cause you shame."

Zillah looked into the instrument, trying to identify the different stars he explained to her, but shook her head in dismay. It was no use. She couldn't make sense of it. At last, he led her to the parchment stretched on the ground. By the bright starlight, she could plainly see the markings on it.

"You see here, and here, and here?" Balthazar was pointing to different marks on the chart. "Can you see that the stars look as though they form two fish? Or, at least, they look that way if that's what you are looking for. That formation is called Pisces, or Fish, as Melchoir told you. And if you could see it, the mark on your cheek looks like this formation. Have you never seen the shape on your cheek, Zillah?"

She shook her head slowly. "Once, my father tried to show me how to see my image in the water at the end of the rainy season," she said. "He told me it's in the shape of my mother's hand. It's the sign of her touch. But I never knew her."

"Ah," Balthazar nodded in agreement. "I can see that if you were looking for it, you could see that shape as well."

For the first time in her eleven years, except when Father took her to find the secret tree, Zillah felt special, someone who mattered. She liked the way Balthazar explained that it was possible to see what you were looking for in the stars as well as in the mark on her face.

She felt so safe with him that she blurted out, "The boys of the serai call me a name—fishface—when they want to be mean. But I don't think they know anything about the stars!"

"They don't know what they are talking about. It is their ignorance talking," Balthazar smiled.

"That's what my father said." Zillah was surprised at herself telling the story. It wasn't safe, in the desert, to tell anyone anything about herself or her life. But Balthazar patted her cheek again, ever so gently, smiled his warm smile, then turned back to his work as she watched.

Time flew by and Zillah, worn out from the long day and her hours of work, was hardly aware that she finally dropped to the shawl the women stretched wide to receive her. The talk going on all around her, the amazing story of the star, and especially Balthazar's blessing of her birthmark buzzed around her head like desert flies.

Slowly, the sounds of the animals in their pens faded. The entire courtyard was still bright as day from the light of the extraordinary star overhead. While the rest of the caravanserai slept, the Assyrians walked about as though it was daylight. But Zillah no longer noticed. Her eyelids were heavy with sleep.

CHAPTER 8

ESCAPE FROM
THE SERAI

Zillah dreamt that she was walking up a bright pathway into the heavens, walking on the beam of light from a huge star. Peace seemed all around her until suddenly she sensed danger. The danger became more real as she heard a man's voice shouting, "Useless baggage, daughter of Belial!"

Then she was falling from the star, falling fast. Her arm hurt, and Zillah opened her eyes to the bright light of the sun instead of the huge star. Her uncle was shouting and shaking her roughly by the arm.

"Disgraceful girl! What have you been doing? Already the sun is high in the sky! Your aunt had to lay out the morning meal by herself while you slept here among strangers. You, lazybones, sleep away the day as though you were a common herdskeeper or a desert rat."

"You will work hard for the rest of the day, and you will have nothing to eat until you pay attention to your work!" he stormed. Zillah hurried to her feet. Her uncle still gripped her arm, and in her confusion, she was unsure whether the stories in her head were true or just dreams.

A king to be born, she puzzled. One who would set people

free. And her birthmark, something special to set her apart! It seemed a strange idea, in the light of the sun.

As she hurried to her chores, she wondered how she had fallen asleep on a strange shawl in the sand, how she had let herself believe those stories. She worried that Uncle might be right, that she didn't deserve to be among these Assyrians.

Aunt called her, "Daughter of a slug! Come and wash the pot from the morning porridge that I had to cook all by myself. You good-for-nothing girl! Why am I cursed with the likes of you?"

Zillah was upset and fearful. Was she wasting her time thinking she could be apprentice to a king, when she was just as surely "daughter of a slug" as Aunt called her? Even so, as she moved about helping Aunt prepare food for other travelers, she could not completely cast aside the astonishment of what she had seen and heard last night.

Her mind kept going back to the Magi, whose presence seemed to fill every corner of the caravanserai with the mystery of their language; the sweet, strong fragrance and abundance of their food; the softness of their clothes. And the star! Their own special star to follow! Their amazing instruments and . . . their astonishing stories! Could there really be such a king?

She hoped for the chance to slip back among the travelers to hear more. True or not, their stories helped her forget the dreary days and nights of her own life. But she had really seen the star, of that she was certain. She could hardly wait for evening, when it would appear again. There had to be some truth to the stories they told, as far-fetched as they sounded.

As the morning wore on, Zillah was filled with a desperate longing, not only to hear more but also to be part of the stories of the Magi. She let herself imagine that they might take her with them, that she could be honored for her special mark in the shape of a fish instead of feared or despised. She wondered if they would allow her to become one of their servants and to travel with them to see this new king.

She daydreamed about a different life as she fed the animals and carried the clay pots of water for cooking. "Perhaps I, too, could learn about the charts," she thought. 'Perhaps I could learn to help plan the journey."

She didn't care that her ideas got bigger and wilder with each bucket of water. She wanted to escape this dreary place and her aunt and uncle, to see the world beyond the caravanserai. What would it be like, she wondered, to follow the star and see this king they were talking about?

She couldn't imagine how that could be possible for her, until she hurried to the south gate to gather more clay tablets for the day's records. In all the excitement of the Magi's stories, she had forgotten the dream her Father had spun about the precious oil and the promise it held for her future.

"Father told me the precious oil was my legacy," she thought. "If it is as valuable as he said, perhaps I could use it to bargain for my escape. Do I dare trust the Magi with this secret?"

She felt a pang at the idea of selling her prized oil, for it was all she had left to remind her of Father. It remained the special bond between them. As she thought about this secret, she was reminded of the image of the stranger in the red turban. It made her afraid and angry at the same time, wondering if he had something to do with Father's death. But she shrugged it off. There was no time to think of the past. She had to try to figure out how to deal with the present—and her future.

The caravanserai bustled with activity. The Magi and their servants and animals were getting ready for the next leg of their journey. And another, smaller caravan carrying salt was almost loaded to go out the gates. Camels and donkeys brayed, and their restless fidgeting stirred up clouds of dust in the hot afternoon sun.

But there wasn't much time to think. Zillah wondered why the salt traders were also leaving at this odd time, but she had to register their departure too. Soon her chance to approach the

Magi would be gone. Glancing about to make sure no one was watching, she slipped away to the hiding place behind the stones at the south gate. She checked to make certain the oil jars were still there. What if the man in the red turban, lurking about, had discovered their hiding place? She held her breath as she searched for them and was relieved to find the oil in its place, undisturbed.

She counted three small clay jars of the oil her father had worked years to save, still uncertain just how she might use them for her escape. Would the Magi accept her offer to exchange oil for a place in their caravan? Would it be too much, or not enough? What if they demanded to know where she got it? And if they accepted it, would they allow her to work as one of their servants to earn the food she ate?

So many questions and no answers, she thought, tucking the small jars carefully away and replacing the covering. She knew she would never go back to the hidden oasis for more—it was a close call the last time. She didn't know how much those bandits knew, or where they might be hiding, waiting for her to lead them to the oil trees if they hadn't already found them.

Zillah gathered her clay tablets and hurried back toward the counting rock. The salt caravan was waiting, the drivers impatient to be off. It did seem strange that they had waited until the end of the day to leave the serai, as most caravans hurried to leave early in the morning. It wasn't safe to travel the desert at night, unless, like the Magi, you followed a wondrous star. And it was strange that Uncle Mahli wasn't shouting for her; he was nowhere to be seen.

The women among the Magi's caravan worked hard to prepare the food for their journey. They would travel from sundown to long after sunup in the next leg of the journey. The men were folding their tents, giving the camels water to carry them through the desert, and gathering and packing their belongings.

CHAPTER 9

A THIEF AMONG US

Everybody in the royal caravan made their preparations in a calm, unhurried way that suggested they knew exactly where they were going and why, and that they would be well prepared. Excitement filled the air. Moving among them, Zillah felt a surge of joy at the thought of joining them, though she still wasn't sure how she would manage such a thing.

As she passed behind the camel stalls, Zillah was shocked to spot Uncle Mahli, head lowered so that she could hardly see him, among the camels belonging to the Magi. Uncle never dirtied himself by working among the animals, and Zillah wondered why he was there now. And why was he was hiding?

Zillah was even more worried when she saw her uncle lift the flaps of the readied saddlebags, poking and prodding inside, lifting out beautiful silks and quickly replacing them. Clearly, he was searching for something.

The guards stood nearby, but their eyes were on the salt traders, a rough-looking bunch. Still, Uncle was risking everything, even his life, if he were caught.

Afraid to look, Zillah peeked again to see Uncle Mahli reach deep into one of the bags, pulling out a handful of small leather sacs. Zillah caught her breath as one of the guards turned his way. But Uncle Mahli quickly returned his find to its rightful place, except for one small sac, which he slipped inside his garment. He pretended to adjust the straps on the largest saddlebag as the guard approached him, sword drawn.

"Ah, you see, this one was not secure," he told the guard. "You should be more careful, for there are thieves everywhere in the desert. I closed it properly so nothing will be lost."

The guard put his sword back in its casing and checked the bag. He looked sharply at Uncle, but said nothing.

Zillah hurried back to her station, worried and ashamed. It was one thing to overcharge, as Uncle often did, but to take something that didn't belong to him? He could lose his hand, if not his life! At the very least, the name of the caravanserai that his fathers had owned would be dishonored.

She was late attending to the salt caravan, but she focused on the work to be done. Now and again, she cast an uneasy glance at the three Magi and their caravan.

As she marked the tablets, counting the salt blocks, the leader of the caravan watched her every move. Zillah was beginning to know most of the caravans that came through—some for the second time since the death of her father. She had seen many of them over the years as she played at her father's knee, then worked beside him. But this group, like the Magi and their caravan, was new to her. And yet, there was something familiar about the leader of the caravan that she couldn't quite place. It was in his eyes, the way he watched her. She felt she had seen him before.

Finishing her accounts, Zillah saw Uncle approaching. She was not surprised to smell his strong breath behind her and to feel the familiar fingers pinching her neck to indicate she should add a few drachmas to the price. Sometimes she pretended to add figures to appease him, but this time she just ignored the pain and finished totaling the columns, charging only what was fair. Finally, she turned to look at him.

"Leave me alone," she said. He looked surprised, but then his face grew red and angry. She thought he was going to hit her. But at that moment, the ochre-robed king strode toward them. Uncle's face suddenly turned from anger to fear. His hand dropped away from Zillah's neck, and he held his hand in front of his face as if to ward off a blow.

Kaspar was furious but his anger was different from Uncle Mahli's. Zillah could feel its force as he approached. While he touched no one, his voice struck as powerfully as if he had.

Everyone in the caravanserai, including the salt merchants, stopped to watch. Zillah felt as though the sun stood still. And the usual bleating and braying of the animals went silent. Even the wind seemed to stop blowing. Uncle Mahli leaned so far back she thought he might fall over.

As Kaspar reached for Uncle, Zillah gasped, thinking Kaspar meant to strike her uncle. Instead, she saw Kaspar reach into Uncle's garments and pull out the small leather sac that he had lifted from the camel bags.

Zillah caught her breath and waited, afraid for what would happen next. Aunt Ahliah was nowhere to be seen, but several of the Magi's guards came to stand on either side of Kaspar, their swords drawn. The crowd gasped and dropped back, including travelers and caravanserai guards, women, and children.

"Kill him!" one of the salt merchants called out.

"Let's see the color of his blood!" a boy shouted happily and picked up a small stone to heave at Uncle Mahli.

But Kaspar's guards kept their swords at their sides as the king opened the little leather bag and took from it a large golden ring with a huge ruby that sparkled in the afternoon sunlight. "So!" Kaspar thundered. "This is the kind of host we have at the Serai Mahli!"

Zillah covered her eyes. It was just what she had feared. Even if they didn't kill her uncle, the caravanserai was disgraced. Every traveler, every caravan would know that this was a place that could not be trusted.

"That's my ring! I got it in exchange for lodging," Mahli lied. "It . . . er . . . it, it is a gift for my wife. I—I—exchanged many goats to win it for her. I had it hidden because it is a surprise."

His eyes shifted around the crowd, looking for support. But the caravanserai workers looked at the ground. They knew that Mahli never had such a ring. And if he did, he would wear it himself, not give it to the unhappy Ahliah.

The salt merchants, who had been about to leave, began to mutter and some picked up stones and hurled them at Uncle, shouting, "Thief!" Others took up the shout, "Kill him! Kill him!" and began to pelt him with stones and camel dung. Even Uncle Mahli's own guards, who were paid to watch the walls and who carried swords, did nothing to stop the stone throwers or to help him.

Zillah was afraid for Uncle's life and for her own. She tried to shout at the mob to stop, but all she could do was stammer, "D-d-d-d-on't!"

Suddenly, Balthazar strode into the circle around her uncle, unafraid of the rough men or the stones they threw. Even more amazing, none of the stones came near to hitting Balthazar. A hush came over the group. Some of the stone throwers stopped with their hands still in the air, the rocks they were about to throw falling harmlessly into the sand.

Balthazar took the ruby ring from Kaspar's hand, looked at it, and held it high, slowly showing it all around the group. When he spoke, it was loud and clear.

"The gods have mercy on your soul, keeper of this caravanserai. You shall indeed pay dearly, but not in the way you might think. As you value this stone, as cold and as hard as your heart, so you shall have it!" He handed the ring back to Uncle Mahli as everyone watched in silence.

At first, Uncle Mahli refused to take it, and Balthazar thundered, "Take it!"

Uncle reached out reluctantly, his hand open, and Balthazar dropped it into his hand, refusing to let his hand touch Uncle's, a sign that he considered him unclean. As Uncle Mahli closed his fingers around the ring, Balthazar spoke, his voice quiet now.

"Take it, for we have many such rings. These were among

the jewels to be presented to the new king, but this one is of no importance. You could have had it for the asking. You value the wrong things. So in exchange, we shall take something that has much greater value before the gods, but that you value very little."

Zillah watched open-mouthed, unable to imagine what the Magi knew of Uncle's possessions. Wise though he might be, how would Balthazar know what the gods valued? Did he read it in the stars? Would he take over the wells and the caravanserai and send Uncle away?

Instead, Balthazar called for Siri. Turning slowly, he gestured toward Zillah. "Come. Help her get ready."

Siri left the group of servant women and came to where Zillah stood, unable to move, and took her hand. Terrified, Zillah wondered what Balthazar meant to do with her. Siri spoke softly to her as she led her to where the other women from the caravan stood. Everything happened so fast; Zillah could barely take it in.

"You can come with us, Zillah," Siri whispered. "Do you understand? I will help you pack your belongings, but we must be quick." At first, Zillah could think of nothing she owned besides what she wore on her back. But then she thought of a small leather bag she kept with trinkets that her father had given her—a small gold chain, a special white rock they found in the desert.

She was glad that Siri ran with her as Aunt Ahliah followed them to the hut she shared with Aunt and Uncle. She was speechless when Aunt came to her and handed her some small coins— ten drachmas.

"You might need this," Aunt said softly. "Be careful, Zillah. And remember all that I tried to teach you." She gave Zillah a quick squeeze around her shoulders—the closest she could come to showing affection.

Zillah hugged her quickly. "I'm sorry to leave you, Aunt," she said. She partly meant it.

CHAPTER 10

ZILLAH'S ADVENTURE BEGINS

Balthazar turned to his companions. "Come," he said. "We are ready to leave." He beckoned Zillah and Siri to join him. "Come, young Zillah. You are now one of us."

Zillah stared at him and smiled uncertainly. Had the Magi really purchased her for the price of a ruby ring—a stone near the color of the mark on her face? Was that her worth to the Magi? To Uncle?

Father would never allow such a thing. To be exchanged for a ring—it was unthinkable. And yet, it made her smile inside that she, a girl who counted for nothing, could be exchanged for a jewel.

She glanced at her uncle. What would he do without Zillah? Who would carry water for Aunt? Uncle Mahli stared at her, his face twisted in fury. Zillah realized she had no choice but to go, now that she was part of an exchange that shamed Uncle in front of the whole caravanserai. At least he was whole. Under the code of the desert, the man from whom he stole had the right to cut off his hand.

She touched the small leather bag at her waist and then she

51

remembered the one thing she did have of value: the small clay jars of oil in their hiding place.

"Wait!" she exclaimed to Siri and her mother. "Oh, please wait for just a gnat's eyelash!" She ran across the caravanserai, no longer concerned about exposing her hiding place. Still, she was painfully aware of Uncle's eyes following her as she slipped behind the rocks and stones at the south gate. Other eyes followed her, too, eyes of dangerous men among the salt merchants. Yet she felt safe in the company of the Magi.

"It's not exactly how you planned it, Father," she whispered, as she stuffed the little jars in the leather bag at her waist. "But this is surely what you would do, if you were in my place."

Uncle Mahli stood in the middle of the compound, almost hidden by dust from the departing salt traders. Zillah ran past him, still afraid of what he might do. Aunt Ahliah now stood a little behind him, looking at the ground. Neither made a move to stop her. Uncle didn't look at her either, but raised his fist defiantly at the Magi, who acted as though he no longer existed.

Even Kohath stood silent for once. Zillah turned for a last look at them and felt a brief pang of regret. She was leaving everything she knew.

"Good-bye," she ventured timidly. "Good-bye, Kohath." Kohath lifted his hand in a short wave, glancing at Uncle as though afraid he would be punished for even that.

"Good-bye, Aunt," she said. Ahliah tilted her head, acknowledging Zillah.

"Good-bye, Uncle," she said last, expecting no response. But he did respond. He spat once, twice, three times. It was done.

She turned to Siri and the other women, who led her to the waiting caravan. Strong hands lifted her onto the back of a camel behind one of the drivers, then Siri behind her. Although she had fed and watered hundreds of the beasts, Zillah had never ridden one. She wondered at the broad back, the strength she could feel beneath her as her legs gripped the sides of the camel. Even the smell was different to a rider than to a water carrier. Everything felt so strange. Was she the same girl who awoke this morning to Uncle's shouts? She touched the birthmark on the side of her face. Could that have changed, too?

As the animal began to move, Zillah felt sad to leave behind the hidden oasis with the oil trees. But she couldn't deny the excitement of the adventure before her. She reached down to touch the little bundle of clay jars to make sure they were secure.

A sharp thrill ran through her. She was following the great star just as she'd wished. And her precious oil was safe for another day. She was going to see this unknown king of the Jews and to find out about the promise to set people free. She was free of Uncle Mahli and Aunt Ahliah. What more freedom could she ask?

The drivers put the camels in loose formation, roped together four abreast. It was strange to look out at the desert from her perch. Other members of the caravan gazed ahead to see what lay before them. But Zillah strained to look as far as she could in every direction.

Seeing into the far distance of the desert from the back of a camel wasn't as awesome as observing the stars come down to earth, but it was like nothing she had experienced. She saw several small clumps of trees, marking the presence of water, even though it might be too far beneath the desert sand to quench a traveler's thirst.

As she stared around her, she thought she caught a fleeting glimpse of Father's hidden oasis. She sniffed the desert air, now fragrant with the possibility of rain. During the rainy season, the desert came alive with white, yellow, and pink flowers and green plants.

Zillah spotted the sun-whitened bones of a camel sticking up through the sand some way off. She wondered about the story of those bones. Father would have had a story to tell, even if he had to make it up. Zillah smiled. She always believed him.

The saddle and bags swayed with each step the camel took, Zillah and Siri along with them. The chains around the camel's

53

necks jingled and the drivers sang songs with strange melodies and words Zillah did not understand.

They rode throughout the night. The silent presence of the bright star above them seemed to signal that everything was going to be all right. Zillah felt her fears slip away. She wanted to see everything, to miss nothing. But the tinkling of the camels' ornaments and the drivers' singing, along with the swaying of the camel, was like a lullaby. Zillah's head gradually dropped to the bundle in front of her and soon she was fast asleep.

When she awoke, she was first surprised at the gentle motion beneath her, thinking she was dreaming. She expected to hear Uncle and Aunt shouting for her to get moving on the day's work. She slowly opened her eyes, remembering that she was riding on a camel with a caravan of people she'd only known for two suns. She had mistaken the beam of the star for the hot desert sun.

Opening her eyes wider and looking about her, she saw the whole caravan bathed in that mysterious light. The star hung so low in the sky, so bright. They were steadily climbing and Zillah could no longer see the entire caravan as they followed steep rises and rounded hills that hid others in the caravan from view. They had left the flat desert behind.

As Zillah stirred, Siri, sitting behind her, called out, "Zillah, are you awake? Doesn't our star look as though we could climb on it, just as we climbed on the camels?"

Zillah laughed. "I'd like to try it, wouldn't you?"

Siri continued, "Zillah, it's brighter than it's ever been. It makes me feel so strange. I wonder what kind of king could have such a star? Sometimes I think we shouldn't have come."

Zillah had no answer, for she, too, wondered whether the star might blind them to possible danger. She hadn't relaxed her habit of watching everything, and twice she thought she saw a flash of light on the hillside nearby.

The caravan kept moving, and as they rounded a hill, Zillah saw the Magi's three camels with their glittering howdahs far ahead, making their way up a steeper rise. They were surrounded by guards on camels of their own, swords glimmering in the star-light. Zillah leaned back against the blanket behind her and tried to relax. Surely there was nothing to worry about.

CHAPTER 11

A DETERMINED ENEMY

Every camel was piled high with a driver and riders, tents and blankets, food and water. Zillah counted the camels as they rounded the hill, pleased that she had learned about numbers from her father.

The Magi disappeared over the rise, and Zillah watched as the others followed. As their own camel approached the pass, she was not prepared for the sight that spread out before her. Glimmering in the early morning light and stretching as far as she could see in both directions was a broad river, wider than any ten little desert streams. A mist rose from the surface of the water, lending it a dreamlike feeling.

She and Siri sighed with relief when the camels were drawn to a halt at the riverside and made to kneel among the harsh tufts of grass so their riders could dismount. They slid off without help, eager to explore this endless river. The grasses that the camels eagerly attacked offered a welcome dampness to their feet, and the morning songs of birds in the trees filled the air with sweet sounds.

"It feels so good to stretch my legs!" Siri exclaimed. "I should be used to the ride by now, but I'm always glad when it's time to stop."

"Let's wash off some of this desert sand," Zillah suggested. The two girls ran, laughing, to the riverbank, joining others eager for a drink and a wash. Everyone was talking and laughing. This was the River Jordan. It meant Jerusalem was not far away.

Zillah wondered what was happening at the place she still thought of as home. Who records the travelers? Do the guards still obey Uncle Mahli after his disgrace? Are they able to see the star? Does anyone wonder about me?

She didn't have much time to think about it because one of the women called out to her and Siri to take food from the baskets, fetch water, and spread cloths where food could be laid out for the hungry travelers. The women scurried about, laying out dried meat with flat bread and cheese, fruits, and nuts. They would not stop long enough to start a fire or to cook the hot and spicy food and drink they had prepared at the caravanserai. The Magi had decided that this was the time and place to cross the river.

Zillah watched the women, uncertain at first how or where to begin. Then Siri called her to help carry water jugs from which everyone could drink. Each woman knew her task, and before long, the meal was ready.

Meanwhile, the men made sure the camels had food and water, brushed them down and checked their feet for injuries. They inspected the camels' loads to make sure they were securely fastened.

The three Magi and the young princes who rode with them ate first, taking the flat bread in their fingers and rolling the meat and cheese inside. They spoke little, but concentrated on their food, eager to resume the journey. After the Magi and the princes had taken their fill, the guards and the camel drivers took what they wanted and moved to the outer edges, near the animals, where they ate noisily, calling out to one another and laughing as they ate.

When the men had eaten their fill, the women and children ate from what remained. To Zillah's surprise, there was still plenty of food and no one was left hungry. While the women ate, some of the men went to the river to fill water jugs for the rest of the journey.

As the women cleared away what was left of the food, the Magi took out their instruments and once more checked their maps and charts. With the great river before them, they needed to make sure of their crossing. As soon as they were done with their chores, Zillah and Siri moved in as closely as they dared.

A young man came over to stand near Siri, and to Zillah's surprise, Siri put her hand in his.

"This is Raveen. We are betrothed," Siri whispered to Zillah. "He is one of Balthazar's guards."

Raveen pulled himself up straight and tall and made a show of straightening the sword hanging at his side. Zillah drew back, not sure she liked this interruption of her friendship with Siri, even though he was very handsome as he smiled down at Siri and then Zillah.

"Don't worry, Zillah," he told her. "I am always careful with my sword. I have been trained in how to use it properly. I've never yet killed a bandit though," he said with regret.

"And I hope you never do!" Siri scolded. "I hope you never come that close to a bandit, Raveen!"

"Well, my master, Balthazar, says that if we do not live by honor and peace, we die by the sword," Raveen said, fingering the weapon at his side. "Of course, it's the job of my sword to help make certain that our enemies give us honor and respect and leave us to our peace." He laughed.

"We are fortunate to have such a wise ruler," Siri told Zillah. "King Balthazar brought peace to the squabbling among our neighbors. And it was he who convinced Kaspar and Melchoir to join us in this long journey."

One of the women walked toward them, and Raveen quickly dropped Siri's hand. "We will be wed in the first quarter of the next new moon," Siri explained. "King Balthazar has determined that the stars show that will be our most favored time for a long marriage and a fruitful one." Zillah smiled to see how Siri blushed.

"We are almost finished packing the baskets for crossing the river," the woman scolded. "And you stand there as though you are royalty, with nothing to do." She turned to glare at Zillah.

"You must earn your place too. You may have caught Balthazar's attention because of your learning, but even you must work to eat."

At that moment, the young man called Zothar approached from around a group of camels, striding toward them as though he had a mission. Perhaps he had been sent to find them. Zillah saw both Raveen and Siri grow tense.

"Zothar is the nephew of King Balthazar," Raveen explained to Zillah under his breath. "He believes he will be heir to the kingdom because Balthazar has only daughters."

But Zothar ignored both Raveen and Siri. He approached Zillah, his shoulders back and his chin high, so that he could look down upon her.

"You!" he said. "Daughter of a thief! What right do you have to travel with the Magi? You are no better than camel dung. In fact, that's what you deserve to eat—camel dung! We will see how the daughter of a thief will fare—you with the evil mark on your face—especially one who thinks she can read the stars!" He spat at her feet, but Zillah stood her ground.

"I am not the daughter of a thief!" she said.

"Your stupid father stole a valuable ring from our king," Zothar sneered, but Zillah interrupted him.

"The man who stole the ring is my uncle, not my father. My father is worth ten of you!"

"So you are a liar as well. Before this journey is over, you will learn that a grubby caravanserai girl, even one who claims to be able to read and write, has no place in the company of our wise and great kings!"

"I don't know what you're talking about, and I don't think you do either," Zillah challenged. "You'd better leave me alone because my father is watching you!"

Zothar whirled, his hand on his sword, and Zillah laughed. "You will not see him, but he is there!" she said.

Zothar turned back, furious. "Try to make a fool of Zothar and you will pay a price, I guarantee! I carry the authority of my uncle, the king. My sword can cut out the tongue of worthless servant girls who cross me." He turned and strode away.

"Pig!" Raveen spat out, careful that Zothar was far enough away so he couldn't hear. "Worse than a pig! Carrion! Fit to be eaten by vultures."

Siri put her hand lightly on his arm. "He is not worth your anger," she said. "He only does that because he knows he is not as good a man as you, Raveen; he's trying to prove himself."

Then she turned to Zillah, her face serious. "You must be careful, young friend. You can see what a temper Zothar has, and he carries a grudge. You do not want Zothar for an enemy. Why did you say your father was watching him? We could see no one was there."

"The spirit of my father watches, I know he does," Zillah defended herself. "Bandits took his life, but I know his eyes still watch over me."

"That was not your father at the caravanserai?" Siri was surprised. "And you have no mother? Then the gods will have to help you, for you have no one to defend you if Zothar attacks. And, Zillah, you are in danger, for you made a fool of Zothar and you laughed at him."

"Ah, I will defend Zillah!" Raveen declared. "My sword is thirsty to defend the honor of a maiden. Especially against Zothar!"

"No!" Siri cried. "You will not! I will not lose you in a fight because this girl doesn't know better than to laugh at a prince."

CHAPTER 12

CROSSING JORDAN

Zillah had never felt quite so alone. Even after Father died and she had no one but Uncle and Aunt and their beatings, she had at least felt secure when she was standing behind the big rock, counting the visitors to the caravanserai. Beatings she understood, and she knew their limits. The uncertainty of Zothar's dark threat was worse.

But now wasn't the time to worry. A sharp call went out throughout the caravan, each camel driver shouting to the next to get the camels ready to cross the Jordan River. Over their hurried calls, everyone saw the clouds filling the horizon, darkening the skies. Heavy rain would raise the level of water in the river and make it impossible to cross, so the cries urged everyone to hurry.

The royal leaders had already gathered their instruments and maps. They were at the river's edge discussing with the lead camel drivers the best place to cross. Raveen helped Zillah climb onto the camel, then Siri. From her perch high on the animal, Zillah looked about for Zothar, but he was nowhere to be seen.

"Maybe Zothar will forget," she whispered to Siri.

"Zothar has never forgotten a slight in his life," Siri sighed. "He always looks for trouble. But I have never seen him pick a fight with a girl before, Zillah. I think he's jealous because of the attention Balthazar paid you. It's not good to have caught his eye!"

Drivers on foot led the camels carrying the kings into the river, step-by-step. The big animals picked their way, edging into the water. Zillah wondered at the way they moved, so carefully, yet so sure-footedly through the swirling water. The water reached just above the camels' knees, and above the waists of the men leading them. As they reached the center of the river, the water was deeper, blacker, and faster. The water came up to the edges of the saddles, soaking the lower-hanging bundles and lifting the men leading the camels off their feet. Had they not clung tightly to the camels' ropes, they surely would have been swept them away.

Ropes linked the next group of camels to the first, but they waited until those first four were safely on the other side. Then the drivers led the second group of camels into the water.

A third group entered the river, but their drivers stayed on the backs of the camels, guiding them along the same passage followed by the first two, and the next group did the same. The first, more experienced drivers had set a pattern for the others.

Just ahead of the girls' camel were the goat-herders and their flocks. At first, the lead goat refused to go. The herdsman leading the goat struggled to make it step into the water. The herdsman was a powerful man and had managed his goat through tough spots before. He held tight to the goat's rope and spoke as gently to it as he might to a child, petting the goat with one hand and pulling it with the other. Finally, the goat entered the river and started to swim across, the herdsman swimming strongly beside it. Zillah, who had only seen goats confined in the pens inside the caravanserai, couldn't believe how willingly the other goats followed their leader. They all swam safely to the other side.

Both girls clung to the saddle when it was time for their camel to move into the river. The swiftly moving water glittered in the sunlight as it swirled around the camel's legs. Looking intently into the water, Zillah could see that travelers before them had built up the riverbed with rocks to form a sort of road so that a camel could walk across if the current wasn't too strong. Still, it would be difficult to cross later in the rainy season.

Zillah held tight to the saddle. Siri, sitting behind her, wrapped her arms around Zillah's waist.

From the first, it didn't feel quite right. The big animal shuddered as it stepped down the riverbank then stopped short and let out an eerie call—the high whine that Zillah always thought sounded like a cry for help. She looked down at the driver leading the beast by its halter; he wasn't their regular driver. Growing increasingly frightened, Zillah glanced around. Their camel wasn't linked to the others, and she noticed that this driver didn't handle the camel with the same assurance as their regular driver. Perhaps that was why the animal was so skittish.

Behind them, the next driver was getting impatient and called out in a loud voice complaining about the delay. The girls' driver made a sharp retort, and then they felt the animal beneath them shiver as it was struck from behind by a well-aimed rock. The animal jumped, then reared, twisting sidewise. It turned toward the river's edge, away from the crossing.

The few camels left on the river's bank began to mill around, loudly protesting. They hadn't been eager, in any case, to plunge into the river. A strong wind stirred the leaves on the trees and whipped the grasses into a frenzy as dark clouds scudded overhead. The camels became even more agitated.

Suddenly, the man leading their camel, who moments before had seemed as though he didn't know what he was doing, expertly swung himself up on the neck of the camel and began whipping it into a run. But instead of crossing the river, they headed along the edge of the river and away from the crossing.

Siri began to scream, and Zillah looked wildly around, trying to understand what was happening. Why were they heading in the wrong direction, back toward the rocky hills? And who was this man driving their camel? Panic stricken, she saw that three other men on camels moved in to join them, appearing from behind a wind-blown clump of trees. Heavy rain began to fall.

Zillah thought she recognized the face of one of the men. She got a closer look and became even more terrified. It was the salt merchant from the caravanserai. She was sure, now, that he was the same man she had seen in the desert wearing the red turban. This wasn't just a runaway camel.

Terror gripped her, but she couldn't make a single sound come out of her throat. Everything was moving so fast that she couldn't think.

The salt merchant was now riding his camel hard, coming up alongside theirs. He leaned out and grabbed Zillah's arm, trying to jerk her off the camel. She clung to the saddle, refusing to let go, trying to shake him off.

Siri was still screaming and holding tightly to Zillah, but the man was too strong. His camel was running faster than theirs, and he was able to pull Zillah from her camel and onto his own.

Pain shot through Zillah's shoulder and down through her arm, but she continued to hit, scratch, and kick her kidnapper. Still, the man held her fast, pinned against the leather saddle. She squirmed and fought to loosen his hold on her.

"I have to keep moving," she thought. "He can't get control of me as long as I'm still moving!" She kept twisting and turning, biting and scratching, refusing to let him get a good hold of her as he urged the camel over the hill and away.

She felt a sharp tug at her waist. The leather band attached to the small leather bag with its treasure was pulled so tight it took her breath away. She realized the man meant to steal her bundle of oil jugs. He cursed as he twisted and jerked it, trying to break the leather cord.

"Leave that alone!" she yelled. "In the name of my father—it belongs to him!" She tried to jab him in the ribs with her elbow, but he wore so many layers of clothing—now soaked from the rain—he didn't feel her punches. The man gave another yank and pulled the bag free.

"It's mine now!" he said with a nasty laugh. With the bag in one hand, he made a fist and punched her. Pain exploded in her temple. He punched again, but this time the blow glanced off the back of Zillah's head. Dazed, she tried to grab the bag back. The man wasn't expecting Zillah to continue to fight, and the movement threw him off-balance. Zillah saw her chance. She grabbed his arm and sank her teeth into his flesh. He howled in a rage and shook Zillah off. He nearly knocked her off the camel and under its running feet. As she was falling, he quickly snatched her from the air and pulled her back across his saddle.

"You will not get away from me until you tell me the secret of the desert that you carry in this little bag," he growled into her ear. "You think a mere girl can outwit Naceraen the Bandit? Hah! Your father couldn't, and you can't either."

At the mention of her father, Zillah's heart all but stopped. She was in the hands of the murderer who had killed her father! But he wouldn't kill her until he discovered the source of the fine oil. That would give her time to get away and, perhaps, to avenge her father's death.

Desperate, she wondered what happened to the others from her caravan. Where was Siri? And where was Raveen with his sword?

CHAPTER 13

THE RESCUE

Zillah fought to loosen the bandit's hold on her so she could see where they were headed. She looked for signs to show her the way back to the river's edge. But as she struggled, the bandit only pushed her down harder. In any case, the rain was drumming on the land with such force that it was hard to make out any landmarks, and the other bandits were riding their camels close on both sides. It was impossible to see around them.

"The cave!" one of them called out.

Much as she would be glad to be out of the storm, Zillah knew that once they were in a cave it would be even harder to get away.

"I have to watch for my chance as they dismount from the camels," she thought. "There might not be another." She wondered whether there would be a way to grab the leather bag with the oil jugs from the bandit. They were her last connection with her father; they gave her strength.

As the bandits neared the cave, a hair-raising cry came from behind and to the side of a pile of nearby boulders.

"Haiiii!" the call echoed all around them. It was like no sound Zillah had ever heard. The bandit was surprised as well, and as he turned to look, his hold on her loosened. She twisted around and grabbed his thumb with both hands and gave it a sharp jerk, as far and as hard as she could. She felt it snap and he shrieked with pain. She grabbed the reins and, using all the strength in her body, shoved him off the camel. He landed on the rocks below, lost among the the running legs of the camels. It was the last she saw of him.

Victorious, but scared and alone on the camel, she tried to rein it in, but she couldn't control the frightened animal. Men on camels were fighting all around her. She heard a heavy grunt next to her and saw one bandit slide off to the side of his camel, blood on his cloak.

Zillah's camel, wild-eyed, made a sudden turn and dashed into some nearby brush, running through spiky branches that grabbed her off the saddle just like the bandit. But this time she fell through the scratchy brush and landed with a plop, on her back. The ground around her felt like it was spinning, and the skin on her bare arms and legs felt as though it were on fire.

She put her hands over her face and curled into a ball, afraid the running camels would trample her. The ground shook with their pounding hooves, and she could hear men running and shouting all around her. She opened her eyes just as the long legs of a camel jumped over her, and she curled into an even smaller ball, shutting her eyes as tightly as she could. She shook with fear.

At last, the rain stopped as suddenly as it started.

She was relieved to recognize some of the voices as those of guards from the caravan of the Magi. When she finally opened her eyes, Raveen and Siri stood over her, both of them soaking wet and looking exhausted and worried.

Raveen replaced his sword in its holder and reached out with his other hand to help Zillah up.

"Careful," Siri said. "She's already bleeding from the thorns. Here, let me help." Siri used her scarf to hold the branches away from Zillah so that she could slip out from among them.

"Oww!" Zillah cried, as her hair caught in one last thorn.

"You were lucky we saw you being kidnapped!" Raveen said, as Siri tried to brush some of the dirt from Zillah's face, hair, and clothing.

"We all came, all the guards that had not yet crossed the river! We had our swords and our knives out. Those who didn't have camels gave chase on foot."

Other guards were now gathering about them, telling their versions of the chase. "Yow!" one of them said. "I've never given chase in a rainstorm before! Those bandits and their poor old maltreated camels were no match for ours. They didn't know what they were up against!" He laughed proudly.

Zillah could only stare about her in a daze. It had started and ended so quickly.

"How many bandits were there?" Siri asked.

"Well, some got away. I saw them running toward the hills. I didn't have time to count them, but they weren't taking the time to look back!" another man said.

"Look," Raveen said, "two of them still lay where they fell. They haven't moved."

As Zillah's head cleared, she remembered her leather bag with the jugs of oil. She cried out in alarm, "My leather bag! The bandit took it!" She started to jump up to run to where the evil ones had fallen, but groaned in pain. Several guards stepped in front of her, and Siri held her back.

"Don't be a fool!" one of the guards scolded. "Just because they are fallen, you can't be sure they are dead. They could rise up and kill you! We're armed, so we'll go first."

To Zillah's surprise and chagrin, it was Zothar who came back with her small leather bag in his hand. He strode over and dropped it grandly at her side.

"Here you are, Zillah, the bag you think the thieves wanted so badly. I hope it was worth all the bloodshed today. I can't believe anything *you* could carry is worthy of such a foolish attack on the caravan of the Magi!"

Zillah hugged her leather bag to her chest, afraid to look inside with everyone watching her. She was even more afraid that she might find the jugs broken. She began to calm when she realized there was no fragrance coming from the bag, a sign no oil had spilled.

"This was my father's, and he told me to keep it always," she said. "It means a great deal to me. Thank you, Zothar." She looked around her and called out, "Thank you all for what you did today."

"And thank you, Raveen," she looked at the young man standing next to Siri. "I'm grateful that you are a well-trained swordsman."

"Those men won't be back," he said. "I don't know how far they'll make it. We spilled their blood, but our leaders teach us not to kill unless our lives are under threat. By the time we finished with them, they weren't a threat to anybody, so we let them live."

Zillah's eyes grew large. She wondered if the bandits would find another way to come after her and her prized oil. As though he could read her thoughts, Raveen laughed.

"Don't worry, Zillah. They won't be going after anyone for a long, long time—if ever. And they certainly won't want to cross swords with us again!"

The group rounded up their camels and started back toward the river crossing. Cautiously, while the others told and retold stories of the fight, Zillah peeked inside her bag. She reached in to feel the small clay pots, to be sure they were still tightly plugged, and to count them—one, two, three. Just right.

As they neared the river's edge, they realized the situation at the crossing had changed considerably. With the passing of the storm, the sun glinted again in the sky. But the river had swelled with the rain. Swift and dangerous, it swirled above rocks now submerged in the heavy water. The travelers could no longer see the raised part of the riverbed where the others had crossed, and no one knew what to do.

No sooner had they realized they had no leader, when Kaspar and two of his guards emerged from some trees around the bend in the river. A small cheer went up from the forlorn group standing at the flooded crossing, and Kaspar smiled down at them from his camel, a smile so wide they could see it from where they stood.

"I'm so glad to find you," he called out. "You were like lost sheep. We had no idea where our flock had gone when you didn't follow us across the river. We had to find another place to cross, to come look for you."

Raveen, Zothar, and the others were eager to tell their tales of rescue, and Zillah was glad to let them. She felt that she caused the whole caravan more trouble than she was worth. She clutched her small leather bag at her side and listened quietly.

Raveen boasted that his sword tasted its first blood that day. "I chased the bandit who carried my betrothed away," he said, "and I attacked him without mercy when he tried to take her in the opposite direction from those who carried Zillah. I'm sure they thought we would all stay together and follow in only one direction. That was his second mistake. Taking Siri was his first." He smiled down at her.

With Siri safe, he had joined the chase with the other men. No one was sure how many were in the gang of bandits.

"But we can be sure they won't be attacking our caravan again any time soon!" laughed one of the young men. The others agreed.

Raveen wasn't the only one who had never been in a real fight. Zothar bragged that he had knocked down two of the kidnappers. "With my spike, I impaled one of them to the ground!" he boasted.

Kaspar congratulated the guards on their quick work, then noticed dried blood on Zillah's arms and face and her bruised cheek.

"And what happened to our Zillah?" he asked. He dismounted from his camel and produced a bag of sweet-smelling ointment from within his cloak.

"Here," he said, "use it on those sores and scratches. It will help you heal."

"She was the one who started it all," Zothar declared loudly. "The bandits wanted to take her—for that small bag she carries at her side. But I rescued it. I should carry it from now on, to keep it safe, if it is so valuable. No girl can keep it as safe as I can!"

Kaspar smiled at them all, ignoring Zothar's claim. "The important thing is that all are now safe. And farther up the river I found a place where we can cross safely. Come. The others are waiting."

The girls climbed back on their camel, their own driver again in place, and the whole group followed Kaspar to a safer crossing. Though the water was still high, this crossing seemed nothing after the terror they had gone through. The late afternoon sun dropped behind the mountains ahead, sending long purple shadows across the travelers' path.

CHAPTER 14

A TROUBLING DREAM

King Melchoir and King Balthazar were busy studying the sky with their instruments when the stragglers reached the rest of the group. Their journey was nearing its goal. The mountains ahead were the last hurdle. A few more days and nights, and they would be at the gates of Jerusalem.

The whole camp was full of excitement, heightened by the stories the young men told and retold of the bandits and their own bravery in rescuing Zillah and Siri.

Zothar loudly insisted on telling the story of the rescue in his own way. But as he did so, Zillah saw that he watched the Magi to make sure they couldn't hear his false boasts. She thought what a coward he was as he blamed her for the attack.

"Zillah brought danger to the whole caravan because of some unfinished business with these bandits from her days at the caravanserai," he charged, full of self-importance. "She is, as we all know, the daughter of a thief. We would be better off without her kind among us."

Zillah started up, angry, ready to challenge his words. But Siri held her back.

"It will do you no good and only make him angry again," she whispered. "Better to let him brag and tell his big stories. Nobody listens to him anyhow."

"But my father was not a thief. He is disrespecting my father's memory!" Zillah couldn't believe Siri was telling her not to defend her father's honor.

"Those who were there know what really happened. You were the real hero, Zillah! You escaped the bandit and made off with his camel, before anyone else got there. They know that, too. But everyone wants to be a hero, not just Zothar. As you see, they don't challenge him, and neither should you. You'll only invite trouble."

Zothar went on with his story. His version was that Zillah's father had sent the bandits to take her back, even though he had kept the ruby ring the Magi had given in payment for her.

"Or perhaps he owed the bandits for some nasty business," he went on, "and they were going to kidnap her to get what he owed them.

"If I hadn't been there—and Raveen and the other guards," he added the names of the others only after they objected, "we would have lost our own sweet Siri as well as this troublemaker from the caravanserai. She bears watching, I tell you!"

Zillah listened in a fury. But she dared not go against her friend's advice. She was, after all, the outsider.

Meanwhile, Siri's mother and the other women came to fuss over her, insisting that she lie back and rest. They wouldn't even allow her to get up to help spread the food for the evening meal. One of them, a young woman with a child of her own, told her the same thing that Siri had said: "Don't pay attention to Zothar's bragging. Everyone except Balthazar—wise as he is in other ways—knows he is full of the wind and blows as he will."

The great star was hanging low in the sky, and it seemed that nothing more could get in the way of their journey. Zillah pushed Zothar and his insults to the back of her mind as she thought about what lay just over the mountains. She had waited so long to learn the meaning of the bright star, and she would actually see the reason for it, a baby born to be "the Prince of Peace."

And perhaps she would be among those to get their freedom.

What did her hurt feelings and aching body matter in the light of this star?

Not everyone in the caravan was thinking about what lay ahead. Most were thinking of their own bellies, and they were hungry. But the Magi were so wrapped up in their work they all but forgot about food. Finally, they told the others not to wait for them—to go ahead with their meal—as they were eager to finish their work. The food they ate that evening was the same as they had every day, but it tasted better than ever to Zillah.

At last, Balthazar announced, "We will load the camels and set out tonight under the guiding light of the star. Before the moon is new, we will reach our destination."

He was so calm. Zillah wondered how he could contain the excitement he must feel after the long journey. After all, King Balthazar had been watching this star for a lot longer than she had, and she could hardly wait. But his way was to take one careful step at a time. He knew exactly what he was doing so nothing was a surprise. And perhaps nothing could make him more excited than the first time he found the star in the heavens.

Zillah was even more aware of how sore and stiff she was as she climbed onto the camel and Siri was too tired to talk any more about their adventure. Both girls fell asleep before they traveled very far.

But for Zillah, it was a troubled sleep, filled with dreams of the threatening faces of the bandits, of Zothar and his flashing sword, and of her uncle's angry face.

The last, most vivid dream featured the glorious star casting a shining path to where Zillah stood watching. Her father appeared from somewhere in the heavens and walked down the path to take Zillah's hand. But, in her dream, she didn't want to go; she wanted to return to the small pile of stones that hid the precious oil at the caravanserai, as though she would be safer near her treasure's hiding place. And Uncle was there, shouting at her that her work wasn't done. On his hand was the ruby ring, but it melted to blood that ran down his fingers and disappeared in the desert sand.

She looked again at the star, and the path was now disappearing. Her father held out his hand, beckoning to her.

She awoke, calling out, "Father, Father," and looked around to see if anyone had heard her. The dream had seemed so real! Was it a sign from her father? She carefully touched the small clay jars at her waist, making sure once again they were still there.

The caravan made its way silently up the rocky mountain trail, winding back and forth. Zillah was surprised to realize that as they moved among the trees covering the mountainside, it wasn't possible to hear the voices of the others as she could in the desert. It felt strangely silent. She wondered if everyone could be asleep. She was glad she could count on the camel driver to watch the trail closely.

Far ahead, where there were fewer trees, she now saw the howdahs of the Magi in the light of the star, leading the way majestically up and around the mountain. Nothing would stop them from making this last bold leg of their long journey.

As she watched sleepily, she saw the lead camels disappearing around the bend in the mountain trail. They were still climbing as the first fingers of light from the rising sun slipped over the mountain behind them. As the sunlight grew stronger, the caravan stopped just before a narrow pass. There, a mountain stream flowed through an opening in the rocks, and the people could drink their fill. They refilled their jugs, while the camels gulped the water.

The caravan rested briefly then hurried on. One by one, the camels proceeded through the narrow pass. As the riders emerged on the other side, they sighed with wonder at what they saw. Ahead of them, across a shallow valley and nestled high in a mountain on the other side, was a city, huge and glistening in the early morning light.

Jerusalem.

CHAPTER 15

JERUSALEM, AT LAST

In the distance, the city perched high on the mountainside looking like a huge clump of buildings growing out of the rocks. What kind of people lived there? It surely looked grand enough for a new king to be born there. As they began to make their way down the side of the mountain, working their way back and forth toward the bottom, where they could begin the climb to Jerusalem, the city disappeared, then reappeared as the caravan rounded the towers of rocks.

What would life be like in such a place? How would they find the child they sought? Questions ran through her mind like the waters of the flooded river. It made the journey easier in some ways, to know their goal stood on the next mountain. In other ways, it was harder, Zillah thought, because she wanted to be there now, to learn the answers to her questions.

Although it had appeared so close, it took several more days to reach Jerusalem. The Magi still checked the star each night and timed their arrival at the city for early morning. In doing so, they joined great numbers of other travelers following the well-worn trails, stirring up clouds of dust as they approached the imposing gates and the guards standing at the entry,.

As they drew closer, Zillah stared in astonishment. Behind the strong walls were towers of every size and description. She saw buildings that had to be made of something other than dull desert clay, for they were of many colors

The walls were neatly built of clay bricks, held together with clay, not the stacked stones and hand-made bricks held together with mud as in the caravanserai. They were taller than four camels might be if they were piled one on top of another. And there were windows in the walls, from which people high above their heads looked down on them.

All around them, people waited for permission to climb the many steps to enter the gates. Zillah had thought she'd seen every manner of traveler coming through the caravanserai. But here there were so many different kinds of people—and more women and children—than ever made the difficult journey across the desert. She wondered if these people were in Jerusalem to be counted, as she had heard grumbling about in the desert serai.

She saw both familiar and strange animals: donkeys, sheep and goats, dogs, chickens and all manner of fowl. She couldn't begin to name them all. And she heard such strange tongues she couldn't imagine how the people could understand each other.

But if she was amazed at the travelers, those people eyed the three Magi and their magnificent caravan with even more wonder. Even though they were in awe of the Magi's group, some of them picked her out, staring at her birthmark. Some pointed and talked loudly about it, making others look. She pulled her scarf closely around her face to avoid their prying eyes.

Most of the people carried heavy burdens on their backs or on top of their heads and looked neither left nor right. But even some of those stopped to stare at the splendor of the Magi and their entourage. Without being asked, people made way to let them pass.

At the gates to the city, the guards were quick to open them wide for the Magi's caravan.

"Do you seek Herod, King of Judea?" one of them asked respectfully. "He is in the city today, we are told, and we have sent a messenger to announce your arrival."

The guard didn't tell the Magi that they really had no choice in whether they would appear before King Herod. The guards were under orders to notify Herod of any unusual travelers. This was a king who didn't like surprises.

Balthazar, Melchoir, and Kaspar conferred briefly, then agreed that in order to find the baby king they must first pay a visit to the reigning monarch. King Herod would surely be able to direct them to the miracle that was taking place under his rule.

First, however, they needed to find a place where they could unload the camels and give them food and water. The visit to Herod could wait until they were ready to make their appearance. They were directed to the largest and finest caravanserai the city had to offer.

As they made their way through the streets, Zillah gazed upward at the buildings, with tall stairways leading to doors above their heads. Then she stared downward, at streets made of brick and stone. It seemed that no one who lived in Jerusalem ever stepped on ordinary dirt.

At the Jerusalem serai, King Balthazar once again took the lead, making arrangements for plots of space where the travelers would raise their tents and roll out their mats. As the camels were counted, the drivers led them to a pool where they could drink.

With so much excitement around her, Zillah hardly knew where to look first. But something caught her eye that she only noticed because of the work she had done at the black rock. The scribes who entered the count of beasts and animals were writing on something quite different from the clay tablets she had used. They used feathers, from which some sort of colored liquid flowed and made marks on flat, thin sheets of material that one could almost see through.

She was drawn to this strange way of writing as she had been drawn to the Magi and the instruments they used to study the great star. She made her way closer and closer until one of the scribes looked up and spoke to her crossly in a tongue she couldn't quite make out. She hastily backed away.

But Melchoir had been watching. He stepped up now and drew Zillah back into the midst of the caravan. He explained the strange writing materials to her.

"Those men are writing on papyrus," he said. "It first came from Egypt, and until now, only the Egyptians knew how to make it, so it was used only for the finest manuscripts. This is a rougher version. It seems that others have learned the process.

"You must have noticed that we use finely tanned skins for our maps and charts. These are not as fragile as papyrus, but the writing on them fades more quickly."

The colored liquid, he told Zillah, was ink made of the juice of berries, or from a sea animal called an eel, much as dye for cloth was made. The hollow feather shaft allowed the ink to flow through it. Zillah itched to take the feather in her own hand and try writing on the strange material called papyrus.

But there were chores to do to get ready for the visit to the reigning king of Judea, whom they hoped would tell them more about the miracle birth. Zillah joined the other women in unpacking fine clothing that had been stored safely from the dust of the desert during the journey. Zillah touched the soft, fine cloth in wonder.

Word spread suddenly among the women that they were to be taken to the baths, a Roman invention built in Jerusalem under Herod the Great. Roman servant girls came to lead them to these baths, and there was a flurry of activity in preparation. The men, they learned, were going to baths of their own.

CHAPTER 16

PREPARING TO SEE A KING

It was a wonder to see water pouring through round clay pipes that passed through the walls at the baths. Water splashed into pools lined with tiles of many colors. Back at the serai, Zillah had never stepped into a pool of water that came past her knees and she never took off her clothing except to wash it. A servant girl showed them how to wrap themselves in special bathing robes to wear into the water while they washed themselves.

But as Zillah waited her turn, one of the servant girls stopped suddenly in front of her and stared at the purple marking on her face. The sight of the mark seemed to upset the girl, for she suddenly turned and ran away. From across the pool, she pointed at Zillah, frowning, shaking her head, and talking in a loud voice to the other servants. Zillah was afraid that she might not be allowed to go to the palace to see King Herod, or visit the baby they sought, because of the purple stain on her face.

She looked about for someone to come to her rescue. But the women from the caravan were too busy with their new bathing experience to notice Zillah. She saw a side door slightly ajar and dashed through it, making her escape.

It wasn't easy to find her way back to where the camels and

the caravan's supplies waited. Zillah was glad she had learned to watch for signs as she walked in the desert. Although the brick-lined streets and the stone and brick buildings all looked alike, she had watched for signs and, at last, she saw the Jerusalem serai just ahead. She ran down the street, eager to retreat to the safety of her own place.

But as she approached, she stopped and stepped close to a wall where she couldn't be seen. Zothar was standing in the shadows, talking to three men whose dusty clothing told her they had just come in from the desert. Why were they hiding behind a clump of trees? She couldn't help but notice that Zothar kept his head low, glancing about as though he was worried about being seen. But what frightened Zillah most was that the men were wearing the same turbans as the bandits from the banks of the River Jordan.

Using her father's lessons on moving about unseen in the desert, she crept up behind them, staying hidden behind walls and trees or bushes. She saw the flash of gold coins handed to Zothar.

"When we have her, we will pay you the rest of the gold," she heard the bandit say.

"You said you would pay me to bring you the little jars of oil she carries," Zothar objected.

"True, but not as much. That would be like bringing us an egg, when it's the hen we need," the man laughed harshly. "We need the girl."

Zothar scowled and said something Zillah couldn't hear. She shrank back into the cover of the bushes. Now she knew for certain why she must not trust Zothar. But it was scary to know she had such an enemy within the caravan of the Magi.

She made her way around to the women's tent, arriving closely behind those returning from the baths. There, they learned that an invitation had been delivered for the entire caravan to attend a feast at King Herod's palace, a magnificent building that loomed over the city. All the women were excited to see inside the palace.

No one asked where Zillah had been. They didn't seem to

realize she hadn't been with them the whole time. The women giggled and whispered, excited about the upcoming party.

Loneliness swept over Zillah. She knew she had to protect herself from Zothar's plans, and she wished she had someone on her side. She didn't know how or when he might act. She couldn't just ignore him, as Siri had advised.

As the women prepared for their visit to the palace, Siri showed off a gown of deep blue with a series of veils that she wound around her body and over her head. "You look beautiful and mysterious," Zillah told her. Siri smiled and twirled again.

Zillah wasn't sure what to do. She had no fine clothes to wear. But then Siri's mother, Jorai, came to find Zillah, her arms full of pretty garments.

"Here," she said, "let me help you find something that will be right for you." She stopped and eyed Zillah, taking in her messy, dirty hair and dusty clothing.

"What's wrong?" she asked. "Why did you not bathe with the rest of us?"

Zillah couldn't bear to look at her, so she kept her head down as she explained.

"A servant girl raised an alarm when she saw my face. When I saw her pointing and talking about me, I was afraid I wouldn't get to go to the palace or to see the baby king. It meant more to me than a bath, so I ran away and came back here."

She didn't dare say anything about what she'd heard Zothar planning. She felt sure no one would believe her.

But Jorai was full of sympathy. "Sweet Zillah," she said, "you must not mind what others think. Those who see the light of the star do not worry about the ignorant ideas of others. Come, you will bathe here, and then we will find suitable clothes for you to wear to the palace."

Shiny and new after her bath, Zillah sat contentedly as Jorai combed her hair. What a new experience! No one had ever combed her hair. And she had never been the center of such attention—trying on clothing, putting on one garment, then another and another until they found just the right one. For a little while, it made her forget all about Zothar and his plans for getting his hands on her father's precious oil.

CHAPTER 17

DINING WITH HEROD

In all the city of Jerusalem, only the temple was greater than King Herod's palace, but not by much. Both were visible over all the other buildings in the city. Each had large square towers on each corner that were visible from every direction, standing even above the trees that grew within the city walls. From the palace towers, watchmen could see in every direction. Herod would receive the Magi at this palace.

Zothar wasted no time in approaching his uncle, King Balthazar, with what seemed like a generous offer.

"I will escort that girl, Zillah," he said, as boastful as ever. "Since I saved her life in the desert, she should travel under my protection. There may be new dangers . . ."

King Balthazar smiled to see his troublesome nephew taking responsibility for someone else for a change. The king looked about for Zillah, but she melted in behind some of the other women, close to Siri and her mother, Jorai.

"Please say that I need to stay with you," she begged Jorai. "I should stand with you and help you as we approach the palace. I am needed here!"

Jorai looked at her in surprise.

"Of course, Zillah! You have always been with us, since we left the caravanserai! Why would we change that?" she asked.

Zillah hesitated. If she told Siri about Zothar, she would say she should just ignore him, as she always did. But surely Jorai would understand the danger once she heard of Zothar's scheme. Looking about to make sure no one else was listening, Zillah whispered into Jorai's ear, "I saw Zothar talking with the bandits. They are the same ones who tried to kidnap me back at the River Jordan. They offered Zothar gold to hand me over. I saw the money! I heard him talking to them!"

Jorai looked puzzled.

"You do believe me, don't you?" Zillah insisted.

"Of course, I do," Jorai said. "But how did they find Zothar among all the members of our caravan? Any one of our men would sooner put a sword through them than deal with bandits!"

Before Zillah could reply, Zothar appeared, making his way through the caravan until he spotted Zillah. He puffed himself up with importance and told her, "My uncle Balthazar said that I should keep watch over you so that you won't cause him further trouble with King Herod," he said. Then he announced so that all the women could hear, "She will walk where I can keep an eye on her."

Jorai said nothing to Zothar, but she put her arm across Zillah's shoulders and said, "Come with me." Zothar had no choice but to walk beside them, or to fall behind. Zillah felt more secure than she had in some time as the Magi and their caravan made their way to the palace.

The three kings rode on the backs of royal mules provided by King Herod. Everyone else followed on foot. Jorai made certain that she and Zillah were always in the center of the crowd, where it would be hard for Zothar to pull Zillah away or push her down one of the crooked alleyways they passed. This made him cross, and he scolded as the crowd forced him to walk slightly behind them—not a place he considered worthy. "Jorai, I am in charge of Zillah, not you!" he said rudely. "She is to follow me, under the orders of my uncle."

Grabbing Zillah's arm, he lectured her. "If you don't stay with me, you will be punished."

"She isn't wandering away," Jorai said, gently pushing his hand away. "She's just fine where she is."

As they neared the palace, men in fancy costumes playing stringed instruments and flutes fell into step beside them. Women in exotic dresses danced along before them, drawing a crowd.

Being part of this parade would have been enough to make Zillah's heart leap for joy had she not been so worried about what Zothar was planning. She memorized markers to guide her back to the serai.

But Zothar didn't try anything during the journey to the palace. If Zillah hadn't heard him talking with the bandits, she might have believed that he was actually trying to protect her. He even acted as though he wanted to talk with her, though he did make certain that others in the group could hear him.

"So, Zillah, this is your first journey to Jerusalem," he said loudly.

She didn't bother to answer. None of them had been to Jerusalem before! Zillah looked about to find Siri and Raveen. Raveen took care to walk apart from Siri, but he stayed close enough so that he could always see her. Zillah was glad she had Jorai close beside her.

At the gates of the palace walls, Zillah kept her head down and made sure her veil covered her birthmark. And she was careful to have people on both sides of her as she passed through the gates.

Inside the walls, she was amazed at the glorious flowers blooming everywhere. Nothing she had seen in the desert prepared her for this. Even more astonishing were bushes cut in the shapes of desert animals and creatures she had never imagined.

Birds twittered in the trees and bushes, their cheerful songs joining those of the musicians. At this moment, the spectacle of dancing women and happy music wrapped in the sweet perfumes of the flowers seemed grander than the mountains at the edge of the desert that Zillah had never tired of admiring.

As they entered the palace yards, they passed a clean, well-kept building that smelled as bad as the animal pens in the caravanserai. She could hear birds chirping and cooing inside the building. Word was passed along, from person to person, that these were Herod's pigeon coops. He raised them as a special delicacy, with meat sweeter than that of geese or other fowl.

The pigeons were beautiful white and gray birds, many of them with pink breasts. And their soft cooing made them sound contented, not like birds waiting to be killed and eaten.

In front of the great palace doors, servants spread purple cloth on the pathway to welcome the three kings. The Magi dismounted the mules and followed the cloth, up the steps and into the grand entry hall. To Zillah's surprise, everyone else was allowed to walk on the beautiful cloth, one that would be worth a fortune at the desert caravanserai!

As they walked into the hall, Zillah stayed back among the women while Zothar, seeming to forget all about her, pushed his way to the front, close behind the three Magi. The girls stared around them, and Jorai explained that the shiny floor and great columns were made of polished marble. Their glowing colors reminded Zillah of the mountains in the late afternoon desert sunlight.

"Indeed, the marble comes from mountains far from here," Jorai answered. "They are made of stone, just as your mountains are at home."

The multi-colored pictures painted on the wall fascinated Zillah, showing the faces and forms of men and women and animals. More colorful pictures covered the ceiling. In here, music reflected from the walls like light, filling the hall and delighting Zillah's ears.

Servants opened the doors to a huge banquet hall, glowing with fire on tall sticks up and down the hall. Zillah, full of questions, asked Jorai about the fires.

"Isn't it dangerous to have fires outside of the fire pit?" she asked.

"Those are candles," Jorai smiled. "They are made of tallow from sheep and the pith of rushes. And they are made to burn inside buildings."

The candles lit the hall as brightly as the early morning sun. It was an astonishing sight, light from the candles, revealing tables covered with cloths as white as the marble in the halls and dancing over the walls, casting shadows here and there. Zillah was glad for the shadows and tried to keep back from the light, her cheek hidden behind her veil.

Beside the tables were long marble benches on which everyone would be seated. But all were instructed to remain standing until the Roman king entered at the front of the hall. As Herod arrived, musicians played and the dancers swirled before him. Herod climbed marble steps to sit on a throne high above the tables. Zillah noticed that although he looked important, he didn't look happy. Beautiful ladies and important-looking men followed and were seated all around him, though none were seated at a level with the king.

This was so different from Balthazar, Melchoir, and Kaspar, who would take the time to explain things to a girl like her, and who walked among the whole group as though they were commoners, even though everyone knew they were the kings.

Herod moved from his throne to a golden table, studded with jewels of every color. He invited the three Magi to join him. The others were seated at long tables just below them. The most honored people sat closest to King Herod's table.

Zillah was glad she was at one of the last tables and that Zothar was far away, on the other side of the hall and closer to the front. She would have no fear of him during the dinner, so she settled in to enjoy the feast. Her attention was soon diverted to serving women arriving with platters of food. For their table alone, there was a platter of cheeses and breads that would have fed everyone at the caravan serai at home! Platters of delicate meat followed that—Jorai whispered that they were feasting on pigeon, such as they had seen on the way. That thought stopped

Zillah at first—did she really want to eat one of those little birds? But the food smelled so wonderful and looked so good, she couldn't resist.

Plate after plate of food arrived, making Zillah wish she could tuck some away for Aunt and—but, no- she wouldn't return to the serai. The thought made her a bit sad, beneath all the excitement around her.

But in her enjoyment of the meal, Zillah forgot about keeping her cheek hidden. A serving girl spotted Zillah's birthmark and dropped a platter of goat meat in fright. Hot juices splattered Zillah and several other people around her.

"What is this mark on this girl's face?" she cried out. "What is she doing here?"

Zillah quickly reached up to pull her veil across her face. An older woman rushed over and, in a soft but urgent voice, scolded the servant girl, sending her to the kitchen. She and several other women did their best to quiet the guests and remove the broken pottery with as little fuss as possible. Then she leaned down and whispered to Zillah, "Come with me, quickly, before King Herod sees you!"

Alarmed, Zillah glanced at the front of the room. But Herod seemed busy in conversation with the Magi. She didn't notice that Zothar was all alert, watching as the woman whisked Zillah out a side door after urging others on her bench to move together, so it wouldn't appear that anyone was missing.

"What are you doing? Where are we going?" Zillah asked, in a panic.

"Be quiet. You are in more danger than you know," the woman replied, pushing Zillah along until she was almost running.

When they were outside of the room, and well down the dim passageway, the woman explained.

"A servant pays with her life for disturbing the king's banquets!" she said. "And you are in danger as well, if King Herod sees you in his banquet hall with that mark on your face. He is deeply superstitious and suspicious as well. He might think you carry a curse because of this mark. You are lucky you were seated far from him.

"It is never safe to be anywhere near this king," she went on, almost as though talking to herself. "Even his sons aren't safe if they cross him. There is a saying, 'It is better to be one of King Herod's pigs than to be his son.'" The woman shook her head in dismay as they hurried along.

Zillah wondered what would become of her, separated from her friends. She tried to stop the woman in her rush down the passageway.

"Wait," she begged. "Can't I just hide nearby so that when the Magi return to the Jerusalem serai, I may join them?"

The woman stopped to consider the question, but as she did so, Zillah saw, out of the corner of her eye, Zothar running down the corridor toward them. Without another word to the woman, Zillah dashed through a nearby doorway and was plunged into total darkness. She didn't know whether Zothar had seen her or not. She felt her way along the wall and crouched behind what felt like a table. She could hear his voice as he questioned the woman. Would she tell him where Zillah was hiding? She waited in agony, expecting any moment to feel Zothar's cruel hand on her shoulder.

CHAPTER 18

ZOTHAR'S REVENGE

The door opened with a bang, and Zillah jumped. She could see Zothar standing in the dim light from the passageway, looking about the room. Now that her eyes were accustomed to the dark, she could see small cracks of light from other doors along the walls of the room. She was in some kind of storage room, with many pieces of furniture stacked about. She shrank back further against the wall, hoping Zothar wouldn't see her.

He came into the room and closed the door softly behind him, standing still, listening. Zillah hardly dared to breathe.

But the dust in the room was too much. She was used to desert dust, which blew about, but didn't settle into her nose like the dust in this room. She felt the sneeze coming and tried to stop it, but it still exploded from her. "Achooo!" Immediately Zillah jumped up and ran around the furniture toward a crack of light she hoped might be another door. Zothar was running hard after her.

He was fast and he was strong, and he reached her as she was trying to find a way to open the door. He clapped his hand firmly over her mouth, lifted her over the furniture, and carried her to the door they used to get into the room.

The servant woman hesitated at the door. Clearly, though, she was not going to help either Zillah or Zothar. She had to protect herself first. What would serve her best would be to have these troublemakers out in the street, and she hurried to show Zothar the door.

"Get out of here," she hissed. "Get out and don't come back, either of you. You will cause me no end of trouble if Herod hears all this commotion. He is already upset about the new king your masters are telling him will come from the Jews. He is in a killing mood. You make yourselves—and *me*—a target with all this commotion. Now go!"

She flung the door wide, and Zothar pushed the struggling Zillah out the door, down the stairs, past the gate and the walls of the palace, and into the street.

When they had gone some distance, Zothar took his hand away from Zillah's mouth, but marched her, stumbling, down the street, a hand firmly on each arm. All the time, he yelled at her.

"Asp of a girl!" he shouted, as he pushed her down the dark street. "You poisoned my future! You made me miss the rest of the dinner and the dancing girls and the wine! You ruined my chance to sit with the King of Judea, among our own kings. My uncle, King Balthazar, will want to know why I left the table. It's all because of you!"

Instead of doing what she really wanted to do—call him a selfish pig and tell him it was his greed and not her that caused him to leave the banquet—Zillah concentrated on finding a way to escape. Her arms ached from his strong grip and her heart beat with fear, still she forced herself to think.

They were on a strange street, different from the one they had followed to the palace gates. She wondered if Zothar knew where he was. She soon found out as he began to curse and look this way and that. Then he shouted again.

"Useless baggage, now you made me lose my way. This isn't the way we came! It's all your fault! I should kill you now and be done with it! And I would, if . . ." He stopped, but Zillah knew what he was going to say: "I would kill you if it wouldn't cost me the bandits' gold." He jerked her arm behind her until Zillah howled with pain. Then she realized that was only giving him satisfaction, as he jerked her arm again. So she bit her lip to keep from crying out, though tears sprang to her eyes. He couldn't see her tears in the dark.

If he had a brain, he would follow the walls of the castle until he came to the gate where we entered, she thought, wondering if she should tell him. If he listened to her advice, she would be in familiar space, too, and maybe better able to escape.

"We could follow the palace walls around to the gate . . ." she gasped.

Zothar stopped, relaxed his grip a little, and looked at her suspiciously. Then he said, "That's what I was going to do, gnat-brain."

"Where are you taking me?" Zillah found the strength to ask.

"I'm taking you to people who will take you back to the desert, where you belong," Zothar sneered. "You don't belong with the Magi. I saw it immediately. You are like a desert rat, hiding under the cactus and stealing treasure where you can."

"What do you mean, 'stealing treasure'?" she demanded. "I've stolen nothing. I've worked for everything I ever got!"

Zothar didn't answer, but pushed her toward the palace walls. Clutching her arm, he marched along the walls, over bushes and under trees and through rough places in the pathway designed to discourage people from passing so close to the palace walls.

The fine clothing that Siri's mother provided for Zillah was torn and dirty by the time they reached the entry gate to the palace yard. But Zothar didn't notice the gate in his anger and was about to move past it when Zillah stopped him.

"This is where we entered," she said. He grunted and pushed her through the gate, past the guards, who ignored them, and down the cobbled street. There were not many people about, and no one to help her.

Clearly, Zothar was hopelessly lost. He didn't know how to watch for those special markings or signs that could tell a person which way to go in the city as in the desert. And she could feel in his grip that Zothar was as frightened as she was—maybe more so, for he did not know how to find his way back to the caravan and his family.

Then, to Zillah's relief, the star appeared overhead, lighting the sky and everything below it. Even more surprising, Zothar seemed not to see it at all. He stumbled and almost fell several times over steps and stones that Zillah could see clearly. She was grateful to the star.

She asked again, "Zothar, where are you taking me?'

"Shut up," he said.

They wandered for a long time. Zothar stumbled along as though his feet didn't quite work, until at last, the stone walls of the Jerusalem serai loomed just ahead.

At that, Zothar seemed to gain strength. He held her arm just as tightly, but in a different way. He walked straighter and taller and pushed Zillah to move faster, though he still stumbled over rocks and stones he didn't see. Zillah felt strangely calm with the light of the star to guide her—especially since it didn't seem to be any help to Zothar.

CHAPTER 19

A STAR TO GUIDE ZILLAH

Once he saw a place he recognized, Zothar shoved Zillah toward the gate of the caravanserai. Now he was watchful in a different way. No longer trying to find his way through strange streets and alleys, he was plainly searching for something.

Zillah soon learned what he was looking for. As Zothar was about to take her through the gate of the serai, one of the turbaned men stepped out of the shadows into their path. Even Zothar jumped back in surprise.

The man was even uglier and meaner-looking than Zillah remembered. Without saying a word, he grabbed Zillah and tried to pull her away from Zothar. But Zothar jerked her back, refusing to let go. She felt as though they would tear her in two. Neither was going to give up without a fight.

"No, you don't," Zothar growled. "You don't take her until I have the gold you promised me in my hands. And if you don't have the gold, I know others who would be willing to pay me that and more to know the source of the precious oil of the desert."

Zillah felt rage rising in her throat, threatening to choke her. These were the men who had killed her father, and they were willing to go to any lengths to get control of the oil tree for which her father had died. Obviously, her father had refused to tell them where the tree was, and she would die too before she would tell them what they wanted to know.

Zothar yanked off the small bag tied around Zillah's waist and held it high over his head, out of the grasp of the merchant. The man leapt forward and tried to grab the bag, and then, to Zillah's shock, another man stepped out of the shadows and punched Zothar hard, full in the face. He went down like a rock and lay flat on the stones, still breathing but not moving.

As he fell, Zillah flew at the man who now held the bag with the little jugs of oil her father had worked so hard to save. Screaming at him, "You killed my father!" she clawed at his face and would have scratched his eyes out if she could have reached them. Surprised by her sudden attack, he tried to bat her away with the hand holding the bag. He missed and slammed the bag against the rocky wall of the serai. Zillah heard the crash and soon she could smell the wondrous fragrance of the oil seeping into the leather bag. The bag and its contents flew out of his hand and slid down the wall, landing on the ground.

Zillah's heart sank. Could all her hopes and dreams end here? She quickly ducked and grabbed the bag in her two hands and opened it gently, praying that at least one jug was still whole. She could feel that not all of the little clay jugs were broken. Two remained. The other spilled its sweetness, and the prized fragrance perfumed the air around her. The bandit reached to snatch the bag, but Zillah was too quick for him. She turned and ran, her heart pounding.

But she didn't get far. With her head down, she didn't see the man rounding the corner of the wall ahead of her and ran into him. "Unnnh!" the man grunted, and Zillah turned to run again until she caught a glimpse of an ochre-colored robe. Gentle hands in ochre-colored sleeves pulled her back, and she heard King Kaspar saying, "Enough, Zillah. You are safe now. We are here." Zillah looked around for the bandits, but they had disappeared. Apparently, they were willing to take on one small girl, but not three kings.

While King Balthazar leaned over Zothar, King Melchoir stepped forward. He breathed in deeply and looked with astonishment at Zillah and the bag she held. Gently, he pried it from her fingers and opened the bag. He pulled out the pieces of the jar that had broken.

"This is some of the most precious oil on earth," he said. "Zillah carried it in her bag!" Zillah stared up at him in fear. She didn't dare move. But she was aware that, beneath her fear was a strange pride that Melchoir sounded impressed by what she carried.

"That's not all that was in her bag," Zothar challenged, now awake, but still sitting on the ground looking dazed. He felt around in his shoulder bag. "She had this ruby ring too," he held a glittering object high over his head. "As I told you, she is a thief."

Zillah saw that it was the same ruby ring that her uncle had stolen from the Magi at the caravanserai. How did Zothar get his hands on it?

"These bandits attacked me because I was trying to defend this lying, thieving girl from the caravanserai, as I said I would do," Zothar said. "How would I know that they were only trying to get back the ruby ring that *she* stole from her uncle after *he* had stolen it from our cargo?

"He sent them after her to get it, and you saw the trouble it caused us all." Zothar looked about him, to see if the kings accepted his story. Zillah caught her breath. She couldn't tell whether the Magi believed him or not. They just stood there, looking at him, then at Zillah.

"I had to leave King Herod's banquet hall suddenly," Zothar went on, groaning slightly as Balthazar helped him to his feet. "Because this little thief slipped into King Herod's private chambers and stole prized oil from the king's treasures, oil he planned to give you to take to the new baby king. She pretends it belongs to her. But where would such a girl get such treasure?"

Astonished, Zillah's anger boiled up in her until she thought it would surely shoot out the top of her head. Would the Magi

101

believe his lies? Would they believe the word of a desert girl against a prince?

Zillah remembered Siri saying, "Don't oppose Zothar." But didn't Siri also say that no one listens to him except Balthazar?

And there was King Balthazar, the man she respected more than anyone besides her father, leaning over and listening carefully to what Zothar was saying.

Zillah could only think to run as far and as fast as she could. She didn't stop to wonder where she would go or what would happen to her. She had to leave.

She didn't want to cause the three Magi more trouble, and she didn't know how to convince them that she wasn't a thief.

Grabbing her bag of precious oil out of Melchoir's hand and clutching it to her chest, she whirled around and ran, sick at heart. Now she would never be able to be part of their world.

She ran back the way Zothar had pushed and pulled her, knowing that he would never be able to find his way to follow her. She heard Kaspar calling her name, telling her to come back, but she ran faster. She zigged and zagged down streets and alleys until she found a small corner where she could hide. She ducked into it and crouched down, quite out of sight, and carefully checked the contents of her small leather bag.

She had guessed right—two small jugs remained whole. She checked their plugs to make sure they were secured and cautiously pulled out the remaining pieces of the broken jug. The fragrance of the oil clung to the broken pieces and to her fingers. It reminded her of the times when she was safe with her father, when they gathered oil from the tree.

"Father," she breathed now, "you have to help me. What shall I do? Where shall I go?"

As if in answer, the star appeared overhead, the star that had guided the Magi over the mountains and valleys, across the desert to Zillah at the desert caravanserai.

"Zillah, your eyes have been opened," King Balthazar had said when she told him she had seen the star as well. And when Zothar brought her back to the Jerusalem serai, hadn't the star guided her while Zothar could not see where he was going?

But now this star seemed to be more than just a guide. She felt a pull, just as surely as if a hand had reached out to her from above. The pull was so strong she stood up, tied the little leather bag to her waist, and stepped out of her hiding place. She looked around and saw no one at all—neither friendly faces nor threatening ones. No bandits in their turbans, no Zothar, none of the Magi.

She wasn't sure which way to turn, but the light from the star drew her toward one of the gates of the city, not the one through which they had entered. It led her away from Herod's palace and the temple.

She followed the pull of the star down streets and alleys she hadn't walked before. She did not watch for special doorways or designs in the walls or any of the other tricks she used to make sure she could find her way back. She was unafraid as she followed the guiding light of the star.

No one stopped her as she passed out the city gate. She was not surprised that she was allowed to pass freely. The light of the star flooded the hills of Judea, and she could see beyond the horizon in every direction. She easily followed the path on which the star guided her out of the city.

CHAPTER 20

AND THE ANGELS SANG

Zillah walked up and down gentle hills and across stretches of rocks. She had no idea how long she had walked, but she wasn't tired. She didn't stop until, suddenly, she heard rough voices nearby and ducked behind some bushes. Peeping between the branches, she tried to see who was there.

She saw a fire burning and men sitting around it, roasting a young goat and drinking wine. Stepping carefully over the rocks and stones so she wouldn't make noise, she drew closer. It was the group of bandits who had tried to pay Zothar to bring her to them!

"We'll find her; don't worry," one of them was saying. "Those rich Persian kings can't keep watch on everyone all the time. Our greedy young friend will find a way to get her out of their sight long enough for us to carry her away."

"It's odd, isn't it?" said another. "He told us they came all this way to look for a child born to be king. How d'you think King Herod is going to take that news?" He snorted, a short, bitter laugh. "Didn't he kill his own sons to keep 'em from comin' after that throne he sits on?"

"Oh, those foreign kings better watch their backs!" said a third man, almost in a whisper.

"Just hope King Herod doesn't have the heads of all of 'em before we get that girl and find out where that oil comes from," the second man said.

"But there is no way to know when they'll leave Jerusalem or which way they'll go," whined another man. "How can we track them when they keep settin' out at night?"

The second man laughed again. "The kid claimed there is a star that guides them."

"Well, they won't travel tonight," said the first. "There's not a star in the sky."

Zillah was amazed, as she was so often, that she could see the star and others could not. She heard the wild dogs howling in the hills nearby and shivered. There was danger in these hills tonight. She hoped the star wouldn't abandon her.

As quietly as she had approached, she moved back through the bushes and clumps of grass, stepping lightly on the rocky ground. Again, the pull of the star moved her forward, though she kept close to the trees and bushes so she couldn't be seen. All her senses were alert for possible danger.

At last, when she was so tired she was stumbling over the smallest rocks, she came to a shallow cave in the hillside, half hidden behind green bushes. Happy to find shelter, she crawled into the space. But as she made her way into the cave, she found the small passageway opened into a huge space.

Keeping close to the wall so she wouldn't risk getting lost, she crawled around a corner to a small niche where, hidden from view, she curled up and fell fast asleep.

Once more, her sleep was filled with dreams that felt like real life. She saw King Herod laughing, his laughter as harsh as the bandit's. He reached for her, his hands dripping with blood. Then he was not reaching for her, but stretching his arms past her to where mothers sat surrounded by small children. Herod's bloody hands reached for the children, and Zillah cried out, trying to warn the mothers of the danger. Her cries woke her, and she was glad to find herself alone in the cave.

But she was not alone. As her senses came alive, she heard movement around her, and she could smell live animals. Then she heard the soft baaing of lambs. She couldn't think where she was. And what were these creatures doing here? She kept still as she tried to focus her eyes. Through the soft morning light now sifting through the cave's entrance, she began to make out the shapes of sheep beginning to stir, tiny lambs nudging their mothers for milk. But she stiffened in fear as she saw movement that became shepherd boys, rising and stretching after a short night's sleep.

She watched them, her mouth dry with fear, and listened to the soft drip-drip-dripping of last night's rain, falling from the leaves of trees and bushes outside. She relaxed a bit as she realized that the shepherd boys had sought shelter with their sheep and lambs after she had fallen asleep.

One, then another of the shepherd boys noticed that they were not the only ones in the cave. They eyed her in wonder, as she stared back. The way they pulled back from her as they stared showed that they meant her no harm.

"Who are you, and what are you doing here in this cave?" one of the older boys asked. "You're not from here, are you?" He looked closely at her, taking in her ragged, torn skirt that still showed signs of the fine garment it had been.

"You're not one of the angels, are you? Lost from the rest of them?" Another shepherd boy squinted at her, trying to see what her clothing might tell him.

Zillah realized that she could understand every word he said, though she was sure she had never heard his language before. But she did not know what he was talking about.

"No, I'm not one of your angels, whoever they are," she answered hesitantly. "I am Zillah, of the desert serai. I came here because I was drawn by the wondrous star . . ." Her voice trailed off as she realized that her story might sound too fantastic to be believed.

But the shepherds did not act surprised. Instead, they began to gather around her, full of excitement and eager to tell their own story. Zillah was the first person they'd seen to tell their exciting news.

"We were all asleep in the field," burst out the smallest boy. "Even Jacob, and he was supposed to be on watch!"

"Shush!" said the boy who had asked if she was an angel, evidently Jacob. "I was NOT asleep, and, anyhow, that has nothing to do with the story. You always want to be the first with every story, whether you know what you're talking about or not!"

Everybody started talking at once, and Zillah could hardly understand what they were trying to tell her. First, each boy wanted to tell her exactly what HE saw, as though he alone had seen this vision. And second, it was about something so strange it seemed she'd never make sense of it. She thought she should ask them to be quiet, in case the bandits were nearby. But there was no shushing them. They were too excited.

"The sky opened up!" said one.

"The light, the light was so bright it hurt my eyes!" stammered another, so eager to talk that his words tumbled over each other.

"We were so scared!" shouted the littlest boy. He came to stand next to Zillah, shaking her shoulder to make sure she listened to him.

"We were not!" objected some of the other boys.

"We were! And you were, too! You were trying to hide behind the sheep!" The littlest boy would not be stopped from reporting what he had seen.

"They were strange beings—more than men or women, or both in one. They were all in white, shining brighter than stars. Brighter than the sun!" Several boys shouted over each other, all reporting at once.

"But they told us not to be afraid!" The littlest boy laughed with joy as he told it.

"They had wings, that I remember," recalled another. "We heard so many wings beating, like many large birds, but with faces like us. And they looked on us so kind. Like my mother almost," he finished in a whisper.

"They were singing," sighed another.

"Yes, singing!" the other boys chorused.

Suddenly, the shepherds were singing at the tops of their voices, "Glory to God in the highest, and on earth, peace to everyone of good will!" Two of the boys broke off with a shout, "Holy, it was holy!" as though they couldn't stop themselves.

The boy called Jacob started to laugh. "The angels sounded better, of course," he said. But the other boys kept shouting and singing. Their faces glowed, and Zillah thought it must be the reflection of what they had seen. She wondered if the star ever made her own face glow, and she was suddenly aware of the birthmark on her face. But none of the boys had said anything about it. None had made fun of her the way that ignorant boys coming to the serai always did.

Just then, Jacob told the others to let him tell Zillah the whole story, from beginning to end.

"We were watching our sheep," he said. "We have to be real careful after dark 'cause that's when the wild dogs are looking for an easy meal, or the bandits are looking to steal our sheep. At first we thought it was an attack. It became so quiet, and then there was the light. We didn't believe what we were seeing—this bright light suddenly split the sky wide open. And all these shining beings—people with wings—came pouring through that split in the sky. There was bright light all around. Their name—angels—came to me, I don't know how. I thought that I was dreaming, and I pinched myself to see if it was real. Then I looked around, and all the other boys were staring at the sky, too. Some fell to the ground, and I thought they were dead. But then they got up again, and they shone, too, like the angels!

"Then the angels said to us—I remember the exact words—'Do not be afraid, for we bring you good news of the best kind, news that will bring joy to everyone who hears it. A baby is born today in the city of David, a baby sent from God.' They said we would find him wrapped in the cloths they put around newborn babies!" Jacob explained.

"So we decided to go to Bethlehem to see what the angels were talking about. We were on our way when the rain came and we took shelter in this cave. And here, we found you—a creature unlike anything we've found before." He smiled to show that he was teasing.

When she finally had a chance to speak, Zillah told them about the star she followed. Their eyes grew big with interest, so that she felt important. But then she felt a pang of sadness as she thought about the Magi who had explained it to her and who had brought her this far. Still, her heart was glad as she told the shepherds about the great kings and the long way they had followed the same star.

"Three wise kings told me this star signals the birth of a baby king whose appearance has been foretold for ages," she said. "This baby king your angels told about must be the same one! The wise kings told me this child will bring peace and freedom to all people.

"But how will we know which baby it is when we get to Bethlehem?" she wondered. "There must be many children there!"

"Oh, it's not such a big town," Jacob said. "But the angels told us something else that is strange. With all the glory that they brought from the skies, they said we will find this child in a manger. Can you imagine? Not even the poorest of us lays a baby in a manger, in a bed of straw!"

Zillah could hardly imagine it, but she was eager to see for herself.

"How far is it to Bethlehem?" she asked.

"Not far—for shepherds, that is. We walk long distances all the time. We might be able to make it this day, if we don't waste time.

"Walk with us, Zillah, if you don't mind being seen with shepherds," Jacob offered. He looked at Zillah's torn and dirty clothing, at the fine cloth beneath the dirt.

CHAPTER 21

ON TO BETHLEHEM

"Are you running from someone?" Jacob asked Zillah, as they walked side-by-side over the rough ground toward Bethlehem. The other shepherds and the flocks of sheep milled around them.

I am running *from* someone, and *to* someone or something," Zillah told him with a smile as they hurried along. She felt freer now that she was beyond Zothar's evil eye, and with the tall young shepherd walking by her side. He understood whom she was running to—whatever awaited them in Bethlehem—but he wanted to hear more about who or what she was running from. She told him about the bandits, how they had tried to kidnap her beside the Jordan River, and how they had trailed the caravan to Jerusalem, where they tried again to capture her. She was pleased at his reaction.

"You were very brave to fight back that way!" Jacob said with respect. "But why were they trying so hard to kidnap you?"

Zillah didn't answer right away. She wondered if she should have told Jacob about her escape. She didn't want to tell him about the precious oil she still carried with her—too many people already knew about it. Nor did she want to talk about her painful split from the Magi. She felt sure Balthazar would believe Zothar's story that she was a thief, and she didn't know how to explain that to Jacob.

She tried to think what she should say. She felt empty without the Magi and her friends in the caravan she had left behind. She believed she belonged with them, and now she would likely never see them again.

Zillah decided to ignore Jacob's question. She smiled up at him and asked him for more details about the marvelous beings singing in the sky. She was thrilled to think that the star she followed was a sign to her, just as the angels were to the shepherds. Jacob seemed willing to respect her decision not to say more about the bandits. He didn't push her to tell more.

But as they discussed these signs in the heavens, Zillah relaxed until she found herself telling Jacob the whole story. He was such a good listener that she told him about her narrow escape near the wadi where the oil trees grew. His eyes grew large as she described hiding in the ancient mountain lion trap and listening for the men to leave.

"What were you doing out there in the hills by yourself?" he scolded, almost like a big brother.

"I felt safe," she answered, "and I was watching carefully as my father taught me to do. I saw them before they saw me! I was there to see if I could find the secret trees Father showed me while he was alive."

At the word "secret," Jacob turned to her, full of attention.

"My father knew where there were precious oil trees," Zillah explained. "He said I must never tell anyone, but I think the bandits were looking for them. I think that's why they killed my father and why they wanted to kidnap me. It's why I fought so hard—it's all I have left from my father. And I wanted to make them pay for killing him. I'd have killed them if I could."

"But they might have killed you!" Jacob said.

"I know, but what is my life worth without Father? Or if I failed to protect his secret? I have no one else."

Jacob smiled sideways at her. "You could stay with us. You'd be an amazing shepherd!"

Zillah was both disappointed and relieved that he didn't ask to see the oil she carried. And it made her smile to think she had earned Jacob's respect. She could be one of them! Telling him the story made her feel as though a great burden had been lifted from her shoulders.

At last, with the afternoon sun sinking toward the horizon, Zillah could see a village on a hillside in the distance. From here, it didn't look like the sort of place where a king would be born. But then, a manger holding straw to feed the cattle didn't seem like the kind of cradle where royal parents would lay their newborn infant either.

"Is that the city of Bethlehem?" she asked Jacob. He shaded his eyes to look ahead and nodded eagerly. His eyes skimmed across the sky, looking for signs of the heavenly messengers they had seen the night before. Zillah looked about as well. She wanted to be the first to spot them—just like the littlest shepherd boy.

She was staring so hard at the city ahead of them that she didn't see the caravan of the Magi approaching on a different path, although the bright colors of their clothing were visible through the trees. The two youngest shepherd boys were the first to spot them and called out in surprise at the sight of the magnificent camels and their riders.

Seeing them gave Zillah a start, and she wondered if she would have to run away again. But she couldn't. Not now. She was too close to seeing the baby king she had traveled so far to see. Besides, Jacob was beside her now, and he knew the whole story.

"Perhaps," she thought, "they will think I'm one of the shepherds." She wished she had asked to wear shepherds' clothing as protection from the bandits, and now from the eyes of the Magi.

But it wasn't the way of the Magi to ignore anyone, not even lowly shepherd boys. As the two groups came together to begin the last climb to Bethlehem, they called out to the shepherds. Zillah sighed in a mix of pleasure and worry to see that Balthazar, on the lead camel, directed his camel to kneel so he could alight and talk with the shepherds. Melchoir and Kaspar soon joined them, and it wasn't long before Balthazar looked at each member of the ragged crew walking among the sheep.

His eyes lighted on Zillah, and his whole face changed. But his look was one of joy.

"Zillah!" he called out. "Zillah! We searched the city of Jerusalem, and we thought you were lost to us! Now, here you are! Come, so I can see that you are well, and that you truly are the desert girl who came with us to Jerusalem because of the great star!"

Melchoir and Kaspar looked up as well, each calling out her name. Zillah thought the singing of the angels could not have been sweeter. Siri, hearing Zillah's name, ran from behind the camels and hugged her.

"Oh, Zillah," she said happily. "This is the best day of my life. I thought we'd never see you again!"

Though she was happy, too, Zillah still looked about for Zothar. He was nowhere to be seen.

But Balthazar was there, and he gently lifted her chin to look at her face. His own was filled with such kindness that it brought tears to Zillah's eyes. Through all her troubles, she had not cried. But Balthazar's gentleness was overwhelming.

"Zillah," he said, "how could you doubt that you would always have a place with us?"

"I'm not a thief!" Zillah blurted. "Zothar . . ."

"We know you are not a thief," he said softly. "We never thought you were a thief. I am so sorry, Zillah, for my nephew's wickedness toward you—and toward your uncle, for he stole the ruby ring from him. I knew it as soon as I saw the ring in his possession. Such wickedness breaks my heart. I hope that he will learn something from this.

"Because of his unrepentant heart, he will not be allowed to go with us to honor this child who has been born in Bethlehem. He will not be allowed anywhere near you."

As though he could read her mind, he added, "And our guards were only too happy to chase the bandits away. They won't be back looking for you."

"You will return with us to our lands, will you not, Zillah?" he asked. "You belong with us." He stopped and looked at Jacob, standing nearby, hungrily listening to every word.

"Now tell us about your new friend, Zillah," he smiled. "And tell us—did he rescue you or did you rescue him?"

"Neither one, master—we all took shelter from the storm in a cave . . ."

Then she noticed he was smiling even broader, and he put both hands on Jacob's shoulders. Jacob looked at King Balthazar with awe.

"You are blessed, too, to find a friend in Zillah," he said.

CHAPTER 22

A KING IS BORN

Feeling accepted again by the Magi, Zillah could no longer contain her excitement about the angels the shepherds had seen. "You have to hear his story," she said. "It is as thrilling as the star that brought us here, and no less a sign from heaven."

The Magi listened closely as Jacob explained that the angels had told the shepherds that they would find the child wrapped in the cloth strips of a newborn baby and lying in a manger. As he tried to explain about the strange messengers that came down from the sky, all the other shepherd boys crowded around, eager to tell the story. Each of them had to have his chance to tell what he saw, for each of them felt that he alone had seen the best of it. All three of the Magi gave their full attention to each shepherd's story, nodding their heads and agreeing that heavenly messengers had, indeed, visited the shepherds

Balthazar walked beside Zillah and Jacob as they climbed the hill to Bethlehem. "We will be returning a different way, and not through Jerusalem," he explained. "King Herod insisted we tell him how and where we find the baby king. We doubted his goodwill, and then last night, in a dream, we were told that the king means only harm to this child."

"I had a dream like that, too!" Zillah exclaimed. "King Herod had blood on his hands, reaching for the babies." She stopped,

suddenly embarrassed by her dream. She smiled shyly at Balthazar. He nodded at her to go ahead and tell her story.

"But when I woke, the lambs were nearby, and I thought he
was reaching for the lambs," she said.

"No doubt that was a warning as well," Balthazar said gravely.
"Now, we are eager to find the baby king for whom we have waited
so long and come so far. We are nearing the end of our journey."

A hush fell on the whole group as they approached the city.
Zillah felt more intensely than ever that peace she had found the
first night when the Magi entered the caravanserai in the desert.
They would soon see the reason for this wonderful peaceful feeling, she was sure.

As soon as they stepped foot inside the city walls, everyone in
the caravan saw the sights the shepherd boys had reported. Hov-
ering in the sky above them were the wondrous creatures clothed
in light. Like the shepherd boys, Zillah heard the rustling of their
wings. And at the sound of their singing, she felt such joy she
could hardly keep it inside. No wonder the shepherd boys burst
into song as they told the story.

The heavenly creatures were not the only source of music,
though. The rocks beneath her feet seemed to be singing, and
songs issued from the mouths of the sheep around her. The trees
vibrated with music. It was all around them.

The light coming from the flying creatures as they sang was
like every color in the rainbow, every beam that ever glistened
from the sun on the most beautiful rocks in the mountain. Zillah
stared in wonder, unable to move.

There, just ahead, was a small shed in the mouth of a cave
that served to shelter the animals. The wondrous star was directly
overhead, and it seemed to encircle the shed in arms of light. Inside, just as the shepherds had said, was the manger full of straw.
Indeed, there were animals all around.

This entire structure appeared to be on fire, but there were no
flames; lights from above danced in joy around the infant lying in
the manger. To Zillah, it seemed that she could see right through

the walls, witnessing the child and his mother, all the animals kneeling in worship.

Zillah fell to her knees. She felt unworthy to raise her head to look at the child or his mother, yet she couldn't take her eyes away from them. The peace she had thought came from the star now filled her heart until she thought she would burst with the joy of it. All the pain and problems of the journey that brought her here were forgotten, as she crept on her knees toward the child.

The youngest shepherd boy didn't notice that everyone else had dropped to their knees in wonder. He ran straight to the mother of the baby. She smiled and drew him to her lap to see the child. He reached down and put his hand around the tiny hand of the baby, and his smile was so radiant that Zillah had to look away.

The Magi held in their hands rich gifts of gold and precious stones and perfumes. They stood back, looking pleased as they watched the shepherd boys crowd around the manger, eager to see and touch the baby. The mother didn't hold anyone back.

A man stood beside the woman, watching her and the baby with tender care. Zillah thought it must be her husband because he looked so proud and protective.

Drawn forward to join the shepherds at the baby's side, Zillah pulled her ragged veil over her face to cover the purple mark, lest she be driven away. But as Zillah raised her face to the baby's mother, the woman smiled gently back at her and pushed Zillah's veil back so that her face was exposed and she could see the baby more clearly. No one seemed to notice the birthmark as the mother nodded toward the baby, inviting Zillah to look at him and to touch him as well.

"We have named him Jesus," she said in a soft voice. "Isn't he wonderful?"

At that, Zillah dared to move closer and to reach out to touch the child. As she did, she felt the small clay jars in her bag bumping against her side, and she knew this was the moment for which she had been saving this precious oil. It was for this child. More, just as surely as her father had told her this oil would purchase their freedom from Uncle Mahli's cruelty, she knew her freedom had already been assured.

Zillah took one small jug from her leather bag and carefully opened it. She breathed in the sweet fragrance. Balthazar knelt beside her, as did Melchoir and Kaspar. With trembling fingers, Zillah handed the open jug to the mother; only then did she dare to caress the baby's soft skin. The fragrance of the oil filled the space where she knelt. The baby's mother carefully poured drops of the oil into her hand, dipped the tips of her fingers in it, and tenderly caressed the baby's forehead.

At that moment the child opened his eyes and looked into Zillah's. Her heart filled with the complete joy of belonging.

His mother reached out and touched her cheek and her birthmark with the oil from Zillah's jug and said, in her musical voice, "You don't need this mark on your face anymore. It has done its work in bringing you here. Your face now is as pure and clean as your heart."

Zillah knew she would never be the same.

ACKNOWLEDGMENTS

Many, many thanks to my family and friends who helped and encouraged me in the development of this book:

Husband, Joe Duffy, chief encourager and editor nonpareil (he loves grammar!).

Family: Tracy and Sharla West, Brady West, Ryan West, and Nicole Gieske, for their encouragement and support.

Friends—writers and editors—Debbie Bennett, Lyn Foley, Kristie Greve, Shirley Halleen, Karen Karstens, Lisa Legge, Gerry McGrane, Alice Negratti, Janice Rehman, Sherry Roberts, Melenie Soucheray, Shannon Toren, Ann Woodbeck, and Jane Yapp, who took time to read and comment as the story developed.

Smart young readers, who approved the manuscript: Linda Stack-Nelson, Alice Ann and Katherine Samuel, Analise Ober, and Trae West.

Mentor and friend, Faith Sullivan, author of *Gardenias, The Empress of One, The Cape Ann,* and other books I love, whose spot-on suggestions made this a better book.

Dara Moore Beevas, my guide at Beaver's Pond Press.

Zillah's Gift is dedicated to our grandchildren: Gordon B. West, Jessie Ella Ann West, Traesha Ann West, and Nicholas G. West.